THIRD LOCH FROM THE SUN

Also by Rex Burke

Odyssey Earth series

Orphan Planet

Twin Landing

Star Bound

Sci-Fi adventures

The Wrong Stop

Third Loch from the Sun

THIRD LOCH FROM THE SUN

A Scottish Sci-Fi Adventure

REX BURKE

ISBN: 978-1-916694-07-1

Cover design: Chris Hudson Design, chrishudsondesign.co.uk

Acknowledgements: As always, my wonderful beta-readers offered advice and support – Sue Bavey, Lisa Rose Wright, Val Poore, Karl Forshaw, Rebecca Hislop and BlueSmoke Bob. I owe a lot, too, to Marion McDonald and Steven William Hannah, who were kind enough to offer an opinion on the use and abuse of Scottish swear words. It turned out that I knew nothing about shotguns either, until Twitter-user Red Leicester put me right.

Chapter 1

He'd give it another five minutes. Maybe ten. Five miles was a long way to walk.

Island time, was that a thing? Jake supposed he couldn't expect everything to run strictly on schedule out here, middle of nowhere.

But the timetable pasted to the bus shelter window was clear enough. The bus should have been here twenty minutes ago to meet the ferry – the ferry that was currently chugging off into the distance, back to the mainland, un-met by any bus.

There was still someone on the otherwise deserted quayside, a couple of hundred feet away, heaving boxes into a Land Rover. He'd watched them being unloaded earlier, half a dozen sealed, cardboard packing cases, dropped onto the concrete as the ferry idled. The Land Rover had driven in ten minutes later, with the ferry already on its way again, and the driver had jumped out and raised an acknowledging hand to an invisible deckhand.

So, island time. All very casual. Great if you lived here and knew what to expect. But Jake was still left with the problem of getting to Port Levin.

The email had said there was a bus. The bus shelter said there was a bus. How long did you have to allow for island time? At what point did you say, "Sod it," and start walking?

Half an hour, reckoned Jake, which was coming up fast. Maybe if he set off, the bus would pass him on the way, turn round at the quayside and head back again? He could flag it down and that would save him at least some of the walk.

There was no point in waiting any longer, for sure. The ferry landing did not have the air of a busy port where alternative transport might materialise at any minute. It was a quayside with a couple of bollards for mooring, a worn metal sign saying, 'Welcome to Elsay,' and a rickety wooden bench that looked out over the water. It was what it was – an arse-end harbour where, also according to the email, the next boat wasn't due for another four days.

Sod it.

Jake leaned over his backpack and adjusted the straps, ready to trudge down the single road that led away from the harbour, towards Port Levin, the island's only village.

On the quayside, the boxes had been loaded into the Land Rover. The engine started and the vehicle swung around the concrete apron and came up the road, past the bus stop. The driver slowed, and then stopped, window down.

"You know there's no bus?"

Jake looked up from his backpack. Young woman, his age, early twenties, long, parted brown hair, a bit of Emma Stone about her. *Easy A* Emma Stone, not *Poor Things* Emma Stone.

"I was beginning to wonder," he said. "Says here there's a bus. To Port Levin, 2.35. It's nearly three now."

"That's not 'To.'"

"What?"

"It's not 'To.' It's 'T.O.' 'Tuesdays Only.'"

"Right." Jake looked more closely at the timetable, but it was tiny print and impossible to tell.

"It's Wednesday today," she said, with emphasis, as if explaining it to an idiot.

"No, I got that," said Jake, thinking – island time is one thing, but waiting six days in a rusty shelter for the next bus was stretching the concept too far.

"And it doesn't run on Tuesdays either anymore," she said.

"What?"

She sighed. "There isn't a bus. Get in, I'll give you a lift."

"You're going to Port Levin?"

"Well, there's nowhere else to go."

Jake threw his bag on the back seat, among a pile of old blankets, a few empty crisp packets, a coil of rope and a well-worn waterproof jacket. Once in the passenger seat – a few plastic drinks' bottles in the footwell – he looked in vain for a seatbelt.

"There isn't one," she said, as she pulled off. "Not mine, the Landy. It's a tip, I know. I keep telling him. One careless owner, and all that. Don't worry, I'll get you there in one piece."

Jake took in the view as she drove up the narrow coast road. Silver-barked trees, and some firs and bracken to his left; stony coves, rocky outcrops, and a sparkling sea on his right. Every now and again there was a passing place for cars, but there wasn't another vehicle on the road. On one stretch they passed a red, triangular traffic sign showing a black deer with branched antlers, the pole leaning back at an angle so it looked like the deer was launching itself into the air.

Far away across the water, he could see the smudge of the distant mainland. The ferry was out of sight. No going back now – or, at least, no going back easily. But it was a warm June day, with a few high clouds, and he hadn't had to walk. No flying deer either. So far, so good. He relaxed into his seat and enjoyed the ride.

"English?" she said, after a minute or two.

"Yes, sorry," said Jake. Sorry? Why did he say *that*?

"Probably not your fault."

He sneaked a look at her. Eyes on the road, straight face, matter of fact. Didn't seem like she was joking.

"No, my parents'," he said, "blame them," but she didn't acknowledge the reply. "Them being English," he elaborated, thinking perhaps she'd missed the point.

Still nothing. Tough crowd.

After another mile or so, she spoke again.

"Did you mean to come here? Elsay? Got on the wrong ferry, maybe?"

"Why do you say that?"

"Nobody comes to Elsay anymore. Not tourists anyway." She made the word 'tourists' sound thoroughly disreputable – the sort of people you wouldn't want on your remote island. Coming over here, cluttering up the place, waiting for your buses, sitting in your crappy Land Rovers.

"I'm not a tourist."

"Glad to hear it because there's nothing to do here. Not anymore."

Jake hoped this was wrong, not least because he had an email on his phone that said the opposite. That specifically said there was something to do here. After all, he'd had plenty of time to memorise its contents on the journey from London – which was now one tube ride, two train rides, one bus ride, one ferry crossing, and one unscheduled Land Rover journey away.

He was, however, beginning to think that the email wasn't fully up to date. There was the erroneous island bus information, for a start. That wasn't encouraging.

And then there was the mention of the 'friendly welcome from the locals, who are always happy to tell you about their beautiful island home.' There was nothing in the email concerning an inquisition by a blunt Emma Stone lookalike. *Cruella* Emma Stone, not *La La Land* Emma Stone.

"Visiting family, maybe?" she said. "The Crowthers have some English in them, I think." She said *that* like 'English' was really not a thing you wanted in you. Like the Crowthers, with their unfortunate anglo-insertion, were to be more pitied than scorned.

Time to put a stop to this. He was tired – it had taken a long two days to get here. He hadn't had anything to eat since a sausage roll at the mainland ferry port, hours ago. And while she was cute, and Jake was grateful for the lift, he wasn't exactly feeling the friendly welcome to her beautiful island home.

"I'm not visiting the Crowthers," he said. "Whoever they are. I've got a job here."

"You haven't." She almost laughed. Scoffed, in fact.

"What?"

This was getting repetitious, but Jake couldn't help himself. It was like she had a special set of nonplussing skills – the ability to come up with a sentence to which the only answer could be, "What?"

"You haven't got a job here. I'd know if you had a job on the island. And there aren't any jobs."

"Well, maybe you don't know everything. I've got a summer job at the Castle View Activity Centre. General assistant."

There was a sharp intake of breath; a drawn out, sub-voiced "Je-sus".

"How did you get the job?" she asked, turning to him briefly, for the first time.

"Website. Then an email with the details. Said I

could turn up any day this week. Said there'd be a bus, too. That's why I was at the ferry dock, waiting."

She didn't say anything for a moment, and then just said, "Website?"

"Yes, a summer jobs' portal sort of thing. Castle View Activity Centre. Do you know it?"

"Aye, I know it," she said, shaking her head, and muttering what sounded like, "Bloody Duncan."

She slowed as they rounded a corner and then, a couple of hundred yards further on, she turned into a driveway, past a weathered sign with missing letters that said, 'Castl View Ac ivity Centr.'

The driveway was spotted with weeds, and the lawns on either side needed cutting. They drove past the main entrance of a white-painted, stone house, with a porticoed entrance. Big front door, two storeys, lots of chimneys – grand in its day, though the peeling paint and stain marks suggested that day was a while ago now. A couple of the front windows were boarded up, and there was a half-filled yellow skip on the gravel outside.

Around one side of the house stretched a low, flat-roofed extension, not quite a prefab building but certainly not the same age or style as the main house. Like it had been thrown up by a local builder with the instruction, 'Keep it cheap.' This, too, looked unkempt – there were weeds poking out of a roofline gutter.

"Staff quarters," she said, pulling up outside. "Door's always open, make yourself at home. There are probably tea bags in the kitchen. And the fridge should be on. I'd check the date on any milk, though."

Jake retrieved his bag from the back seat, and stood there, uncertain.

"Go on in," she said. "It's fine. When you're settled, it's Duncan you want. He can sort it all out."

"Is he around? Where will I find him?"

"Oh, he's not here. He'll be in the hotel, by the harbour. A mile up the road. You can't miss it."

"What time should I go?"

"Whenever you want, he's always there. Be harder to find a time when he isn't."

With that, she put the Land Rover in gear and started to reverse.

"Wait," said Jake. "What's your name?"

But if she told him, he didn't hear it, as she crunched the vehicle back over the gravel and disappeared down the drive.

Chapter 2

Jake tried the handle and pushed at the door. It gave an Addams-Family creak and opened onto a lounge room with a couple of shabby sofas, an old pine coffee table, and an oak dresser against one wall.

There was a big map of the island, Elsay, on another wall, and a cork noticeboard with what looked like a rota or timetable pinned to it. When Jake took a closer look, he saw it was dated from two years previously. There were a couple of yellowing cuttings from a local newspaper stuck to the board, too. 'Lucky escape!' said one of the headlines.

He brought the email up on his phone.

'Your live-in accommodation,' it said, 'is casual but comfortable. Socialise in the lounge with your fellow staff members. Use the well-appointed kitchen to make communal meals – and make new friends!'

Jake looked around, sniffing the musty air in the

room. He didn't think any staff members had been casually and comfortably socialising in here for a while.

The kitchen was sited off the lounge. A stand-up, four-hob cooker with oven, a fridge-freezer making gurgling noises, and some tatty wooden wall-cupboards with a stack of mismatched crockery and mugs inside. A kitchen table with score marks and cup rings. A stainless-steel shelving unit with some old pots, pans and catering trays. He supposed it might be considered well-appointed for a prison-barge kitchen – or, to be fair, any of the student flats he'd lived in over the last couple of years.

The email was by no means finished with its upbeat assessment of the staff lodgings at the Castle View Activity Centre.

'You will have your own* bedroom (*shared with a maximum of three other people). Wake up in the morning to an island view like no other!'

There were three bedrooms down the corridor, each with four bunk beds. They all had a front-facing window and thus, technically, a view – and, given they were bedrooms on an island, also technically an island view. Jake wasn't qualified to say if it was like no other, although as it was of a driveway, an overgrown lawn and some trees, he suspected not.

What it definitely wasn't was a view of a castle, but by now Jake was beginning to get the measure of the Castle View Activity Centre.

So far, no castle, no view, no sign of activity, and – a

mile from the village, apparently – not in the centre either.

He dropped his backpack on a random bunk bed – no obvious bed clothes or pillows – and slumped on one of the lounge sofas, pushing away a couple of dog-eared brochures.

Yes, this probably was all his own fault.

He'd left it late to look for a summer job, annoyed with himself that he hadn't got it together enough to apply in winter for the American summer-camp internships that some of his friends had landed. He'd already suffered taunting messages from Colorado and California, and had stopped checking the Insta clips of toned, tanned figures posing in front of jagged mountains and deep-blue lakes.

And then he'd had to stay three weeks later than everyone else to finish up an assessed module that he'd let drift. All Jake's mates reckoned that Film Studies was a doddle, but they didn't have to explain in five thousand words the significance of four-hour, new-wave, Bulgarian industrial documentaries from the 1970s.

All of which had left him in early June, with no plans and no job – and Jake desperately needed a summer job.

He could have gone back to his parents, and the small seaside town where he had grown up, to stay in his old, childhood bedroom and work in one of the cafés for minimum wage and no tips. But he knew the soul-destroying way that would go, and then he'd have to kill himself and his parents and the café owners and all their customers. That was only going to be asking for trouble.

Instead, he'd taken one final trawl through the websites and forums, and out had jumped 'General Assistant, Castle View Activity Centre, Isle of Elsay, Scotland, flexible start in June, would suit student.'

As far as Jake could see, it only featured on one student-jobs website, which was probably why there were still vacancies – plus the fact that it was a long, long way from anywhere.

He'd looked it up on Google Maps and blanched when he saw it was going to take him six days to get there, then realised he'd clicked the 'walking/cycling' tag. Not that it was a whole lot better by public transport – two days, with a night in a Glasgow hostel on the way, so that he could get to the ferry port for what turned out to be a twice-weekly service from the mainland to Elsay.

But if all that had put other people off, Jake saw it as an opportunity. He'd never been to Scotland, let alone a Scottish island. The place looked amazing from the photos, it was a guaranteed three-month contract, and the pay wasn't bad.

As for 'General Assistant,' it seemed to be a support role at a family activity centre – cleaning and gardening, helping maintain the equipment, a bit of kitchen work, and plenty of free time to explore.

He'd filled in an online application and a return email pinged straight back, with a welcome from a

Duncan Fraser (Director), and detailed instructions on how to get there.

'Don't worry about calling to confirm,' wrote Mr Fraser, who didn't provide a number in any case, 'because the phone service is patchy on the island, and anyway – we always have vacancies. If you'd like to be part of our happy Castle View family, just turn up!'

Jake looked around the lounge again. No sign yet of any happy Castle View family. Could it be grand talk by Fraser, who would turn out to be running the whole show himself? Not that any of this looked like a thriving business, or even a struggling business. It looked dead, shut down, closed.

Castle View Inactivity Centre, in fact.

But he had come all the way here, and still needed a job, so maybe Duncan Fraser, who the girl had said was always at the hotel in the village, would be able to shed some light on things?

There was no door key in the lock, which gave him slight pause for thought until he realised there was probably no need for one. It didn't look as if anyone had been in here for months. He closed the door behind him and set off for the short walk into Port Levin, which he suspected, whatever the email said, was not going to be an 'idyllic harbour settlement overlooking sparkling waters where porpoises play.'

In the event, twenty minutes later, as he rounded the corner to the harbour, Jake was forced to admit that Mr Fraser wasn't entirely full of crap.

Port Levin was picture-postcard pretty, with a couple of rows of cottages set around a horseshoe-shaped harbour, with blue – even sparkling – waters beyond. No sign of a porpoise, though Jake wasn't entirely sure he'd know one if he saw one. Same as a dolphin? Boats were tied up at the quayside, where there was a stacked pile of lobster pots and some skeins of blue netting. A couple of seagulls, perched on a low wall, launched themselves into the air as he approached.

A few larger houses sat back on the hillside, which was topped by the ruined walls and truncated tower of the famous castle. Not a chance you could see it from the activity centre, but at least it existed.

Woods stretched inland, beyond the castle, while heather-topped cliffs rose on the far side of the harbour, obscuring any view further up the coast. It was rather lovely – unexpectedly so, given the rundown state of his lodgings.

As he reached the harbour itself, passing a few of the cottages, Jake could see that it wasn't entirely the idyll it first appeared. Some of the buildings looked a bit down at heel – peeling paint, scuffed front doors – and while there was a small general store, it had a notice on the window that said, 'Open tomorrow (maybe).'

There was one more shop, Fraser Souvenirs, also closed, with a window display that consisted of a pile of thousand-piece jigsaws of Big Ben and the Houses of Parliament, a candelabra made of glued-together shells, and tins of shortbread emblazoned with the slogan, 'Welcome to Edinburgh.'

The Port Hotel was at the other end of the harbour, under brooding cliffs, and it looked a bit shabby, too. The name on the front was weatherworn, and there were dusty bottles in the bay windows. On one side, a conservatory overlooked the water, but the glass was streaked and needed a clean.

It wasn't quite 'The Slaughtered Lamb' out of *American Werewolf in London*, but Jake just knew that when he went in, everyone would stop talking and look at him like he'd molested someone's prize lobster.

He went through the door marked 'Public Bar' to find only one person in there, sitting alone at a booth for four. Man in his mid-fifties, with greying hair and a close-crop beard, wearing brown boots and a wax jacket – like they'd poured George Clooney into Captain Birdseye. He was tapping at an iPad, nursing what looked like a pint of red wine.

Jake had a quick look around. No one behind the bar, no one else in view.

"Mr Fraser?" he said.

"Ah, she said you'd be along. Sit yourself down. Now, it's like this…"

Chapter 3

What it was like, was – there wasn't actually a job, though Jake had managed to work that out for himself already.

"See," said Fraser, "I've had the place up for sale for the last year. There isn't the trade anymore. Isn't much of anything here anymore. Nearly gave it up a couple of years ago, but we tried one last summer, last year. We even had a few families, and a few lads and lasses, like yourself, come here to work. But not enough to keep it going. Not enough to keep the bank manager happy. So, like I say, it's up for sale. And there isn't a job."

"Why did you advertise one then?"

"Ah, well, about that – "

"Because he's a bloody idiot who forgot to take down the online ad and cancel the auto-reply, even though I told him to last September and have been reminding him ever since."

It was the girl from the Land Rover, who had appeared through a swinging door at the back of the bar. She stood there with her arms folded, sporting a just-try-me expression.

"Ah, now, darling – "

"Don't darling me. I told you this would happen if you didn't take it down."

"I forgot, all right? I've had a lot on. Anyway, he's the only one that's turned up. I'll take it down today." Fraser pointed at his iPad and waggled his finger, as if that would somehow magically remove the advert that had dragged Jake six hundred miles to a non-existent job.

"A lot on? Please," she muttered under her breath.

"It's you," said Jake, without thinking, realising that made him sound like the sort of bloody idiot that she appeared to be used to. "I mean, you work here?"

"I work lots of places," she said. And then, seeing Jake was waiting for more enlightenment, "I'm Alva."

"Jake, nice to meet you."

"And the idiot's Duncan – Duncan Fraser, my dad." She shook her head, unsmiling, as if still coming to terms with the fact that she was related to him.

Her dad? Of course he was. One big, happy, Castle View family? Yeah, right. One-man operation, as predicted. Or rather, one-idiot operation.

"Mr Fraser," said Jake, holding out his hand, but wondering where this bad news left him.

"Call me Duncan." The man smiled broadly. "Everyone else does." He nodded theatrically at Alva, put down his iPad and took a long drink from his glass. "English, are you?"

This again. "Does it matter?"

"No, not to me," said Duncan. "I just mean, you've got further to go to get back home."

"I can't go home!" said Jake, more forcefully than he intended. "I need a job. That's what I came here for."

"Ah, well, as I say, can't help you there. No families, no business, no general assistant required."

"Jesus, Duncan, you'll have to do better than that," said Alva. "Listen to his accent. How far do you think he's come? That's southern England, that is. You'll have to pay his fares back, at the very least. How much have you spent to get here?"

"I dunno exactly," said Jake. 'A hundred, hundred and thirty maybe."

"There you are then," said Alva to her dad. "That's your starting point. Hundred each way. Least you could do."

"Now, darling, let's not be too hasty." Duncan looked pained at the prospect of parting with two hundred pounds. "Maybe I can work something out," and he reached for his iPad again.

"You're not going to find a job for him on there," said Alva. "And you're not giving him one of mine."

Jake watched the to and fro with some amusement, despite the circumstances. He had absolutely no idea what was going on, but Alva was giving no quarter and

Duncan Fraser seemed to be flinching under the barrage. Jake might not currently have a job, but at least he wasn't getting both barrels from a disdainful Emma Stone.

"No, no," said Duncan. "Nothing like that. Maybe he can help me with the Castle View? You know, tidy it up a bit and that? It's been empty all winter and spring. The agent said we'd get a few more viewings now that summer's here."

"The agent's stringing you along. No one's been to see it for ages, I wouldn't hold your breath."

"That's because it needs a bit of work. And, er, English here can help me."

"Jake."

"Right, Jake. What do you say? Help me fix it up a bit, do some painting? Clear the rooms, bit of gardening?"

"General assistant?" said Jake.

"Ah, well, no, not exactly. Nothing as formal as that. Day labourer, that sort of thing."

"And what does a day labourer earn?"

"I'll have to think about that. But you can stay at the centre – for free, mind – and I can sort you out with a few quid here and there, if you help me with some other bits and pieces?"

"What kind of bits and pieces?"

"Don't ask," said Alva. "Honestly, you'll be better off getting a couple of hundred quid out of him and going back, getting a proper job back home."

"Alva, let the lad alone. He's got to stay a few days anyway, until the next ferry. Let's see how it works out. What do you say, Jake?"

Jake reckoned he had nothing to lose. Duncan was right, he had to wait for the ferry in any case, and if these 'bits and pieces' turned into a job, it would be a whole lot better than going home to become a waiter-slash-mass murderer in an English seaside town. His only current alternative employment possibility.

Alva shook her head and kept her arms crossed. It was clear she didn't think much of this idea.

"We'll soon have the old Castle View looking better," said Duncan, perking up now the immediate threat to his wallet had disappeared.

"You know you can't see the castle from the centre?" said Jake. "Why is it called that?"

"Don't even go there," said Alva. "Another of his stupid ideas. I've told him a million times. I'm the one who has to explain it to everyone, when they complain about the view. The lack of a view."

"You could see the castle when I was a boy," said Duncan. "Before the trees grew. The name gives it a bit of grandeur, that's all."

"It's misleading," she said. "Like the advert. Like everything you put your hand to. I wish, for once, that you'd – "

"What, darling?"

"Nothing, and don't darling me."

"Right, that's settled," said Duncan. "Come back

tonight," he said to Jake. "We'll talk about it then. And Alva will give you dinner here at the hotel, won't you darling?"

Alva just scowled.

Chapter 4

Back at the activity centre, Jake poked around his new lodgings. Under instruction from Duncan, who had told him where to find them, he unearthed some bedclothes and a duvet from a cupboard in one of the dorm rooms.

"Don't mind the smell," Duncan had said, "It's – " and then he'd tailed off into another digression about where to find the master switch for the oven, so Jake never found out what the smell was. If he had to guess – and putting the best possible spin on things – it was like the bedding had been stored next to something stale, rather than next to something killed horribly and hidden in a cupboard. He hung the sheet and duvet from the slats of the bunk, and opened the room window to let in some much-needed air.

To be fair, the staff quarters weren't too bad. There was power and hot water, a functional bathroom with shower, a working fridge – even the promised tea bags.

"I stay down there now and again," Duncan had said. "To work on the old place. Or, you know, if it's a bit frosty at home," and he'd nodded at the door behind the hotel bar, through which Alva had disappeared again.

Jake could imagine. He'd only met Alva twice, but she certainly seemed capable of dropping the mercury to the extent that you'd feel more comfortable on a musty bunk bed in an abandoned activity centre than in your own home.

Once he'd unpacked, Jake took another look at the island map pinned to the wall. He'd already tried his phone – no reception – and searched in vain for a WiFi connection, so he resorted to some old-school orientation.

Elsay was not a big island, maybe eight miles long by three at its widest point, and aligned southwest to northeast. The one island road, leading up from the ferry landing, ended at the sole settlement, Port Levin. Jake traced his finger on the map up the five miles or so to the harbour, where the road finished. The hotel was marked on the map, and there looked to be a steep, zig-zag path that cut up behind it, onto the cliffs, but then petered out.

Other tracks ranged across the interior down to otherwise inaccessible bays, but the only other road was a narrow one that veered off into woodland just before the village. This curved around behind Port Levin and reached the head of a narrow sea loch on the other side of the cliffs. Not much more than an inlet really, ending in what looked like a small, curving beach.

He looked at his watch. Not yet six, too early for dinner courtesy of the Frost Queen, he suspected. And he wasn't in any hurry. A stroll, then, to get his bearings?

Jake left Castle View and followed the road back towards the village, this time noticing the minor road to the left that narrowed to single track as it ran into the woods. A couple of miles, he had reckoned from the map, through the woods and around to the head of the loch. Thirty minutes on foot, maybe, if he got a move on? He'd have a quick look at the beach, before heading back into the village to the hotel for dinner.

In the event, he got about a mile before he had to stop. The narrow road soon deteriorated, the tarmac patched in parts, before it became more track than road. Even so, it was perfectly walkable – and, indeed, driveable, if occasional tyre marks in the verges were anything to go by.

It wasn't the condition of the road that stopped him, but instead the wooden gate across it, with post-and-wire fencing stretching off either side, deep into the woodland.

Jake looked to see if there was a way through, but the gate had a chain on it and there was a red and white 'No Entry' sign fixed to the bars. He wondered about climbing over – it couldn't be more than another fifteen minutes or so to the loch, and the map had shown the road running all the way there.

But more worrying were all the other signs – on the gate and along the fence for a few yards in both directions. Homemade and hand-drawn, most of them, though sprinkled with a few more official-looking 'Private' and 'No Entry' notices. The homemade ones said things like, 'Keep Out Now!' and 'You've Been Warned,' and – more inexplicably – 'You Can Laugh,' 'Bastards,' and 'You'll See.'

He stood by the gate for a few seconds. It was silent under the trees – or rather, not exactly silent in that creepy way that woods have. A rustle of leaves here, some scratching, the call of a distant bird. And then a loud, single cracking sound somewhere to his left, and much closer than you'd want a loud, cracking sound in a creepy wood to be. Like Bigfoot had stepped on a branch, prior to leaping out and snacking on a human.

Out of the corner of his eye there was a flash of movement. Jake swivelled his head. A vague brown shape flitted in the mid-distance and was then lost among the trees. Try as he might – standing stock still, squinting – he couldn't see the shape again.

He remembered the road sign from earlier. Probably a deer. Probably not Bigfoot, though tell that to his heart.

Either way, that was enough for Jake. He'd seen *The Wicker Man*. The proper Edward Woodward *Wicker Man*, not the dear-god-make-it-stop Nic Cage *Wicker Man*. And there were the bizarre notices. Bad things awaited people who ignored warning notices in creepy woods. That was the rule – anyone who had ever watched a movie could tell you that.

The loch and the beach could wait for another time, or maybe there was a different way to get there, rather than hiking through Chainsaw Massacre Wood? He'd have another look at the map.

Heart still racing a bit, Jake turned and almost trotted down the road – no shame in that – back towards the village.

By the time he reached the Port Hotel it was after seven, and there was music coming from inside the bar. Live music, by the sound of it – he could hear furious fiddling, a couple of duelling guitars, and a strong voice with a determined edge to it.

It was empty inside, apart from a folk band hammering away in one corner, the voice belonging to a thick-set man with a shaved head who was lost in the song, fists clenched as he belted out the lyrics. Something about the 'lost fleet of Spain' and a 'wreck that caused pain,' and then, if Jake had understood correctly, a lengthy account of the many and varied ways that 'pernicious Albion' was to blame for everything.

Jake stood at the bar and looked around, as the band continued to play. No sign of Duncan or Alva. Musicians aside, he was the only person there.

He leaned over to look behind the bar but couldn't see anyone. The song the band had been playing morphed into another, without a break, and Jake looked back at the room, resting one arm on the counter. It seemed rude to walk out again, and a bit weird to go and sit at one of the tables in an otherwise empty bar, but the band showed no sign of stopping, and there was no evidence of any bar staff.

One of the fiddle players looked up from a particularly frenetic piece of bow work, and Jake caught his eye and nodded. The other fiddle player took over, and Jake tapped his fingers a few times on the counter in time with the beat. Slowly, the tune disintegrated as the fiddle ground to a halt, followed by the twin guitars and, reluctantly, the singer, who stopped mid-chorus – mid-word even – as the music faded behind him.

The singer turned to look at the band, some of whom shrugged. He walked slowly towards the bar, wordlessly, laser eyes fixed on Jake, lifted up a hinged counter, walked through, and stood behind the bar.

Quite big, Jake now realised, the singer. Big and intense, solidly built. Like a giant potato with crazy Jack Nicholson eyes. Looming was probably a better word for what he was doing behind the bar. Definitely not just 'standing.' Rearing. Towering. Something like that.

"Aye?" he said to Jake, deliberately, stretching the word out to half a dozen syllables.

"God, I'm so sorry, I didn't mean for you to – you know – I mean, I wasn't – "

The man continued to stand there, impassively.

"Erm, right, sorry. I'll have a lager then. Please."

"You won't. Not in this pub."

"What?"

"Lager. We don't have it, do we lads? Terrible southern drink."

There was a murmur of assent from the band.

God. It was like every bar scene from every bad horror movie. And how was lager wrong? It wasn't like he'd asked for an appletini.

"A beer, then?"

"English?"

"What?" Jake badly wanted this exchange to be over. Didn't even want the drink, but couldn't see any way to back out now. And yet here he was, about to apologise again for something beyond his control. Stupid parents, with their inconsiderate nationality.

"English or Scottish?" said the man. "The beer?" He pointed at the row of beer pumps, and then up at a blackboard behind the bar, where ales were divided into two lists, 'Foreign Beer' and 'Proper Beer.'

Top of the foreign-beer list was a light Cornish ale called Little Widdle. The badge on the tap had a picture of a urinating child. There was no way Jake was ordering that.

"What do you recommend?" he asked, playing for time, but the man was already pulling on a pump further down the bar, filling a glass with something dark and forbidding. Jake sneaked a look at the brand badge and the blackboard. The beer was called Highland Berserker – the tasting notes just said, 'Good Luck.'

The guy put it on the counter, looked Jake squarely in the eye as he reached for his wallet, and said, "Pay later."

"You're sure?"

"Aye son, don't worry, you can't exactly hide on the island. I mean, you can try…"

There was a laugh from someone in the band, and the bartender made his way back as the music started up again. He picked up the chorus faultlessly, and Jake took his drink to a table, crippled with embarrassment.

Five minutes later, the band called it a day, and from the back and forth, Jake realised he'd interrupted a warm-up session for later that night. Ten minutes after that, the bar started to fill – the folk-band singer now firmly ensconced behind the counter, dispensing drinks with an air somewhere between bonhomie and suppressed rage.

Duncan appeared at Jake's shoulder. "What's that, the Berserker?" he said. "Good man, you're a brave one."

"I didn't get much of a choice."

"Ah, you've met Jimmy, then? Gives it to everyone, their first time in. Reckons it's a test of character."

"What happens if you don't like it, or don't want it?" Jake was interested to know because his own tasting notes at this point were, 'Jesus, is that mud? Christ on a bike.'

Fraser looked puzzled. "No idea. No one's ever complained. I mean, you don't want to fall out with the landlord, on a tiny island with the one pub."

"He's the landlord? I thought he was in the band?"

"Among other things. Jimmy McPherson, licensee, taxi driver, undertaker."

"There's a taxi?" Jake couldn't picture it, an island this size. He didn't even want to know about the other thing.

"There's his Land Rover."

"The one I got a lift in with Alva?"

"I wouldn't let Jimmy hear you say that, it'll be on your bill. Right, shall we eat?"

Chapter 5

Fraser led him to a table in the conservatory dining room, overlooking the harbour. Eight o' clock in the evening, early June, it was still broad daylight this time of the year, and Jake gazed out at the sparkling waters beyond the sea wall.

"No porpoises?" he said to Duncan, who had plonked himself down opposite, with another hefty measure of red wine in a pint glass. "Your website mentioned porpoises."

"Ah well, about that," said Duncan, reaching for what was clearly a signature phrase. "Funny thing, used to get them all the time, swimming right up into the harbour. Haven't seen a single one for three, four years now. Migration and feeding patterns, that's what Alva says. Shame, though, used to like seeing them here."

"And the centre? Castle View? Closed down for a year now, you said?"

"More, if I'm honest. Last summer wasn't really a success. We hadn't had a good year in a long time."

"What happened?"

Duncan took a long drink. "Difficult to say, exactly. Couldn't put my finger on one thing, but the island itself is not doing so well. Fewer tourists each year. It's a long way to travel and there's not much here. The salmon used to come up the sound, on their way back to the rivers to spawn, so we used to get the fishing crowd. But the salmon numbers are way down, too. Global warming, says Alva, but I don't know. Could have been the tsunami."

Jake wasn't sure he'd heard correctly. "The what?"

"Tsunami. Oh, it was famous, round here anyway. On the local radio and everything. Not a proper tsunami, you know – big wave, more like. Came out of nowhere, four years ago, one night. Rolled down the sound while we were all asleep. Freak conditions out in the Atlantic, they reckoned. Or after-effect of a meteorite hitting the ocean, they never really got to the bottom of it. Anyway, it washed half a cliff away further north, took out a couple of moorings. We had a lucky escape, the sea wall kept it out of the harbour." Duncan gestured out of the window.

"The newspaper cutting?" said Jake. "Pinned up in the centre. That's what that's about?"

"That's it. Most exciting thing to have happened here in years. They even sent a photographer. Anyway, since then, no salmon, no porpoises. Obvious, when you think about it. Then the ferry company dropped the number of sailings last year, that didn't help either. Just two a week now. And the activity centre – well, you've got to have activities, if you want people to come. We used to have a whole load of great things to do, and then – "

Duncan paused, as if there was more to say, but saw Alva coming into the dining room, carrying dishes.

"Ah, here she is. What's on the menu tonight, darling?"

"You know what's on the menu. You eat here every night."

"Best restaurant on the island," said Duncan, winking at Jake.

"Stop it," she said, putting down two large bowls of steamed mussels. "I'll be back with your chips, but I've got actual, paying customers in the bar tonight, so you might have to wait a while." She gave them a glare. "And you can get the poor man a proper drink, Duncan. He's never going to finish the Berserker."

Jake waited until she had gone back into the bar.

"She calls you Duncan. Not dad?"

"She's always done that, ever since she was five years old. She heard someone say my name one day and latched onto it, never changed back. Strong-willed, you'll have noticed. Then, when her mother died – Alva was eight – she looked after me. Has done ever since. I think it's always been easier for her, that I'm Duncan, not dad. Especially when she's very disappointed in me. Which is most of the time." He winked at Jake again.

"I'm sorry, I didn't know about your wife."

"Don't be. Long time ago now. Anyway, was harder for the girl than for me. I'd had fifteen years with Anja, but she'd hardly got started. Poor wee thing."

Jake ate his mussels – sautéed with onion, garlic, *chorizo*, cherry tomatoes, a hint of chilli pepper, and a slug of red wine, according to Duncan. Minced parsley on top, homemade bread to soak it up. A change from his usual pasta-pesto or Pot Noodle – things were looking up.

"Oh, she can cook," said Duncan, appreciatively. "Got that from her mother. Always helping out in the kitchen she was, could hardly reach the counter. Got everything from her mother, to be honest. Looks, brains. I can see it, even if she can't."

Over coffee, he laid out a few of the things Jake could help him with at Castle View. Put it in better shape, make it more attractive to prospective buyers. There were still rooms to clear in the main house, and perhaps a coat of paint required here and there. The lawn needed mowing, and the flower beds at the front weeding. General stuff, nothing that needed any specific experience, which was just as well because Jake didn't have any.

"Can you handle all that, Jake?"

He could, and even if he couldn't he wasn't going to say. This was beginning to sound like a job after all.

"Only," said Duncan, "I have a few other little businesses to attend to, so I could do with the help. Bits and pieces, but it all takes time, you know?"

"What sort of business?"

"Oh, this and that." Duncan waved his hand, vaguely. "The hotel here, for one," he finally offered. "I have a stake in it. Bought in, when Jimmy's room bookings dried up a few years back. Thought it might be a good investment, but then the ferry timetable changed, and well, you know how it is? Anyway," he brightened, "it still might turn out all right. You never know."

Jake looked around at the dining room. It had a great harbour view, but the furniture and paintwork were tired, and the carpets frayed. And no one else had come in.

"Oh, they won't be eating in here tonight." Duncan had seen his face. "Band night. It'll be busy in the bar, and Alva's serving in there. The whole village comes, as a rule."

"Band night? You mean with the folk group, whatever they were?"

Duncan checked his phone. "What date is it, second Wednesday of the month? That's right, it'll be The Strangle Bunnies."

"The landlord's band is called The Strangle Bunnies?"

"Folk-punk, he calls it. Just one of his bands."

"There's more than one band on Elsay?" That seemed hard to believe.

"No, there's only the one band. Jimmy and his mates, two fiddles, two guitars. Jimmy's the singer, not bad either. First Wednesday of the month they're thrash-metal – Kill Them All, they call themselves. Old

Mrs Dunmore from the shop likes that one. Second Wednesday it's the folk-punk. Next week, they do Eighties covers – Phoney M, they are then. Fourth Wednesday, it's – what is it, Alva love? The other one?"

"Funk and soul," said Alva, who had appeared from the kitchen to clear away the dishes. "He wants to call it The Average Shite Band but Mrs Dunmore says if he does, she won't put the poster up in the shop."

"You've got to love Jimmy," said Duncan. "Don't know what we'd do if the hotel closed."

"You'd lose even more money than you already have," said Alva.

"Don't start, darling. It was an investment, you know that."

"Gamble, more like. I wish you'd have discussed it with me first. I might have had other ideas."

"The island is going to pick up again, you wait and see. Especially if you'd – "

"And don't you start, Duncan." Alva did a bit more of her speciality glaring and bustled out of the dining room.

Jake felt like he was watching a soap opera that he'd caught halfway through season seventeen. There were nuances and undercurrents that he just wasn't getting, in a combative father-daughter relationship that seemed fraught with half-expressed sentiments. It was all very confusing, never knowing if you'd said the wrong thing by mistake.

Not to mention the alarming presence of the brooding, intense, thrash-folk singer-cum-landlord whose right side you needed to keep on if you wanted anything alcoholic on this island.

And Jake had the feeling that alcohol was going to be required if he was to stay on Elsay for at least the next few nights.

————————————————

Chapter 6

————————————————

Jake spent the next two days clearing out the rooms in the main house at Castle View.

Duncan had already removed and sold anything of value – sent it to an auction house on the mainland – which left Jake with the job of rolling up musty rugs, taking down curtains, and filling the skip with bric-a-brac and broken furniture. He took a broom to the bare floors and corridors, throwing up clouds of dust that flickered in the shafts of sunlight through the windows.

Duncan had bought the property years before – another of his investment opportunities – and had run it, quite successfully it seemed, as an activity centre for a decade or more. The rooms were large and light, a good size for families, and various outbuildings had housed the gear and equipment. Bikes, kayaks, climbing ropes, archery targets and butts, wetsuits, wellies – all sold off now, though Jake found a few items in dark corners and cupboards that had been missed. He gathered those together in one of the old barns and made an inventory for Duncan.

Jake slept in the staff quarters – a bit more habitable now he'd cleaned the bathroom and kitchen – and took his meals up at the hotel. A help-himself cereal and toast breakfast, sandwiches for lunch, and whatever Alva had prepared for dinner.

She and Fraser didn't live at the hotel – they had one of the larger houses on the hillside, under the castle – but they might as well have done. Fraser was always there, usually with pint of wine in hand, and used the public bar as his office. The booth table by the window was his regular spot. He had mentioned his stake in the hotel, which Jake supposed gave him the right to come and go.

Alva seemed to be something of a housekeeper. She was certainly always there at mealtimes, either cooking for the bar or dining room, as on Jake's first night, or putting together a meal for her dad, Jimmy the landlord, and now Jake.

There didn't seem to be a Mrs Jimmy, although – because the landlord was terrifying – Jake assumed there had been one and she was now buried under the floorboards somewhere.

Invited by Duncan to 'make himself at home', and use the hotel's kitchen and bar, meant Jake had more contact that he would have liked with a man who, on their first meeting, had told him in threatening tones that there was no escape. Jake had made sure he had paid for the pint of Berserker, and not even balked at the clearly made-up amount, but it hadn't made their awkward encounters in the landlord's home any easier.

There was the music, for a start. Jimmy's breakfast playlist – whether coincidental or intentional – included a lot of strident folk songs whose main topic seemed to be the murdering of the cowardly English in varied and inventive ways. He felt like Monty Python's 'Brave Sir Robin' – another student film society standard – and said as much to Alva, who merely raised her eyebrows.

"Ah, Jimmy's a lamb," she said. "I wouldn't worry, it's not just you. You should hear what he says about the Norwegians."

"A lamb? If you say so. What have the Norwegians ever done to Jimmy?"

"Tried to invade the isles in 1262. He's still cut up about it."

Jake looked at her but couldn't tell if she was joking or not. Though as she didn't seem like the joking type so far, he guessed not.

On the third day of his stay, Duncan came down to the centre to see how he was getting on. He admired the almost-full skip, and walked through some of the rooms with Jake, picking out a few more things that could either be junked or sold.

"Ferry's coming today," he said. "But what do you think about staying on a bit longer? I feel bad that you came all this way for nothing, and I could do with some help with a few things."

"Like?"

"Well, carry on here, for a start. I need it looking better than this to take some more photos for the agent. Lick of paint. Tidy up the grounds."

Jake had been giving this some thought. It hadn't turned out at all like he had expected, but it wasn't the worst job he had ever had, and the surroundings were spectacular. Some of the locals were weird, when they weren't downright hostile, but Duncan, for all his ducking and diving and hopeless optimism, was at least friendly and welcoming. Just as his defunct and otherwise misleading website had promised.

"And maybe this'll help you decide," added Duncan, handing him a hundred pounds in cash. "I told you, bits and pieces when I can, and free board and lodging. You can't say fairer than that. All right? Good man. Now, I'm off down to meet the ferry for a delivery, and I'll need you at the gift shop on the harbour in a couple of hours. OK?"

So, that was that. Employed, at least for a while longer.

Jake walked up to the village later, still enjoying the route and the view as he rounded the corner, with the harbour, cottages and castle laid out before him. There were definitely worse places to have a job, however temporary it might be.

With the right filter on his shots, it would all make a better story for his mates, too, who were currently – and annoyingly – going to lakeside parties with American college girls. Unless American summer camps had changed, or the TV shows had been lying, they were not spending their time filling a skip with old newspapers, broken wine glasses, and pillows with alarming stains, and being glared at by a semi-hostile waitress.

The general store was open for a change, with the old lady, Mrs Dunmore, the thrash-metal fan, standing in the doorway. He waved at her as he passed, and she waved back, so that made at least one person on the island who didn't mind his natural affliction of being English.

She leaned into it, in fact, and called out, "Tally ho!" at him, as she did every time she saw him – seemingly under the impression that, when he wasn't studying the role of death, faith and family dynamics in the films of Ingmar Bergman, he was donning a pink coat to chase foxes through the backstreets of south London.

Jake had been in the shop a couple of times to find it surprisingly well stocked, in the basics at least, and had been able to buy bread, milk, coffee and a few other things for the kitchen at Castle View. The shop also sold tins of lager, so presumably Mrs Dunmore wasn't as cowed by Jimmy as he was. She did, after all, have a fine selection of Slayer and Megadeth CDs next to the digestive biscuits – probably didn't frighten easily, despite being white-haired and five foot nothing.

The gift shop, Fraser Souvenirs, was also open – or, rather, the door was open though the shop itself was empty. Jake called out, got an indistinct reply from somewhere out the back, and then got distracted by the displays.

They were extraordinary, and not in a good way – and not even in the bad way of truly terrible gift shops, where at least the gifts and souvenirs made sense. In that they had something to do with the location of the shop.

Fraser Souvenirs, though, had the most random selection of gifts for sale. They weren't even all Scottish – Norwegian trolls, jigsaws of bucolic English scenes, a shelf-full of Eiffel Towers, Japanese fans. Even when they were Scottish, they were largely promoting Edinburgh and Glasgow, though there was a table of crudely painted stones labelled, 'Locally made by an island artisan.'

"Oh, it's you." It was Alva, her of the indistinct reply, seemingly unimpressed by Jake's presence in the shop.

"Wait, you work here as well?"

She didn't reply, simply pointed up at the shop sign behind the counter that said, 'Fraser & Daughter, Souvenirs.'

"It's – an interesting place," said Jake, filling the awkward silence. Then, without thinking, "Who orders all this stuff? And who buys it?"

"Who do you think, and no one, in that order."

"Right." Jake cast around for something positive to say and alighted on the painted stones. "They're – erm, nice. Who's the island artisan?"

"Who do you think?" said Alva again, before changing the subject, sparing Jake. "I thought you'd be leaving today on the ferry?"

Perhaps it was just her tone, but she sounded almost hopeful.

"Well, your dad, Duncan, came through with some money for clearing up the house. Says he's got some more work for me, too. That's why I'm here – he told me to come to the shop. Anyway, I'm going to stay on a bit longer."

"How much did he give you, for clearing Castle View?"

"Hundred pounds. I was surprised really."

"Figures," said Alva. "Bangkok said he'd do it for two-fifty. You've gone and undercut the island's DIY handyman."

Not for the first time, Jake felt himself swimming in unfamiliar waters.

"Bangkok?"

"Ewan, you'll have seen him in the hotel. One of Jimmy's guitarists. They call him Bangkok Ewan."

"Because – ?" said Jake, when no explanation was forthcoming.

She sighed. "Because he went to Thailand once on holiday."

"Right, of course." Jeesh, island humour. Not exactly *Live at the Apollo*.

"Went to Pattaya, not Bangkok. Dancing on the bar on his first night, he fell off onto one of those low, teak tables. Banged himself hard, you know, on his – " and she gestured in a general downward direction. "Let's say groin. Spent a week in hospital, with the swelling, and when he came back, the idiot told everyone what had happened. Bangkok Ewan ever since. Not to his face, obviously."

To make sure he got it, Alva gave the name the requisite pause in the middle. Bang-kok Ewan.

Jake tried not to laugh and failed. "Brilliant," he said. Even Alva half-smiled, though she reined it in again immediately. God forbid she should show a softer side and, in fact, she was soon back to her old matter-of-fact self.

"He's got you here to help with the delivery, has he?"

Jake looked blank.

"It's Saturday," she said. "And ferry day. The one time we might actually get some visitors, day-trippers. He'll have ordered some more crap from the mainland, too, and gone to pick it up."

"Shouldn't he try and sell all this stuff first? If he can?"

"Well, now you're thinking like a regular, normal, sensible businessman. Not like Duncan, who can't resist an internet bargain."

Jake looked around at the shelves and racks of alpine snow globes, felt leprechauns, New York fridge magnets, miniature boomerangs, Vatican City priest calendars, Costa del Sol tea towels, keyrings with dangling plastic elephants, Tube map underpants, furry handcuffs, personalised Swedish-name novelty mugs, nodding Chinese cats, and plastic Texan stetsons. There had to be entire factories in the Far East dedicated to supplying Duncan Fraser of the Isle of Elsay.

If he ever stopped ordering things, the economies of several major trading nations would take a huge hit.

"Here he is," she said, as a van drew up outside. "Don't say anything. Whatever he's bought, it's not worth it, but he won't be told. Just put it where he wants, and we'll hide it all away when he's gone."

———————

Chapter 7

———————

Duncan reversed the van so that the rear doors were facing the shop entrance. Painted on the back, across both doors, were the words, 'Souvenir Sales & Mail Order,' and underneath that, 'Fraser & Daughter.'

Jake watched from the doorway as Duncan got out and opened up the lefthand door, to reveal a pile of boxes inside. The righthand van door, still closed, now said –

'Mail Order

Daughter.'

Jake laughed and turned towards Alva. "You know that the van says – "

Alva raised her eyebrows and widened her eyes in a manner that suggested that she knew exactly which idiot had painted the van, and what it said, thank you very much, and what was his point?

With nothing else to do, Jake ended up staying at the shop for most of the afternoon. He helped Duncan unload and brought the boxes into the storeroom at the back. One was stamped, 'Made in Albania,' while two more rattled in a way that suggested there were probably more pieces inside than there should be. Jake wasn't surprised. He'd seen how freight was thrown off the ferry onto the harbourside.

Duncan got him to change some of the displays and put out the new stock. The Albanian box turned out to contain fifty pairs of purple, hand-knitted socks, with the Albanian flag embroidered on the big toe.

"Let's put those there," said Duncan. "Get rid of the leprechauns for now. I thought they'd sell for sure."

Jake couldn't see how anyone would think any of this would sell, but Duncan, it turned out, had a plan.

"All souvenir shops are the same," he said. "Especially in Scotland. Tartan this, Nessie that. Kilts, the saltire, bagpipes, all that stereotypical guff. I thought, what about a souvenir shop with souvenirs from everywhere? You know, make a thing of it, a feature? Get known as that shop with *all* the souvenirs? Become a destination retail experience."

"And how's that working out, Duncan?" said Alva, packing the leprechauns away.

"Early days yet, darling, early days. But I've got a Facebook page now, so it's only a matter of time. I just need one of those influencers to get hold of it. Merch, swag, product drops, that's where it's at."

Alva rolled her eyes and said, "Please don't say those words ever again," but Duncan was already on the move, heading back to the van.

"See you in the hotel later," he shouted from the driving seat. "Saturday drinks, all right?"

Jake stuck around for another hour, stacking boxes in the back room, while Alva sat behind the till, occasionally issuing instructions. He heard the doorbell tinkle a few times and was even more surprised to hear the sound of a ringing till.

"Two Eiffel Towers, a cuddly kiwi, and a tin of Edinburgh shortbread," said Alva, as she eventually locked the door at five pm. "The ferry waits for a few hours on a Saturday, so we usually get some day-tripper cyclists up this way at least. Luckily, this lot had an eye for quality international tat."

"Not much to show for an afternoon, though, is it?" said Jake, gesturing at the till.

"Are you kidding? That's the best Saturday of the year so far."

"I don't get it. Won't even cover your wages."

Alva laughed in that mirthless way Jake was beginning to recognise. And which, on this occasion, he understood to mean – wages? Are you having a laugh?

He lingered by the door. "Can I ask you something?"

She inclined her head. An invitation. Go on.

"Why are you here?" said Jake. "Or, how come you're still here? I haven't seen anyone else on the island your age. Our age."

"No school," she said. "You have to board on the mainland. Then most go on to college and don't come back. You've seen the place. Nothing to do."

"But you're here?"

"I live here, it's my home," she said. "What's the problem?"

"I mean, didn't you want to go to college? Or want to stay on the mainland, maybe? There doesn't seem to be anything here, for someone like – "

"Someone like me? And what is that, exactly? What am I like?"

Jake had been going to say 'young, bright, intelligent,' though 'hostile, cross, combative' were also possibilities. Anyway, she was giving him the full, double-barrel Emma Stone at this point, so Jake backed off.

"I didn't mean anything by it, sorry."

"How do you know I don't go to college? Don't I seem the type? Not clever enough?"

"No, god, sorry, it's not that. You seem to have all these jobs here, I just assumed – I don't know, that you've chosen to stay. And I wondered why?"

"Very observant. That'll be your college education, I suppose." She stood by the till, arms folded. "Maybe it suits me? Or maybe I have commitments? Ties? You think of that?"

"I know your mum died, your dad told me. That must have been tough. I guess it's hard to leave."

Jake was busy trying to rescue the conversation and thought he was being sensitive. But Alva shook her head dismissively, like he'd stomped in with his size eleven trainers, making everything worse.

"What's my mum got to do with it? I hardly remember her."

"Stayed for your dad, then? Although he seems like he'd cope, if you weren't here. He's very resourceful, I'd say. Full of schemes, anyway."

"That's part of the problem," Alva said, unguarded, almost to herself. Then she regrouped and changed the subject. "He'll be waiting up at the hotel. They all like a drink once the ferry's away. Go on now, I'll lock up here. I have dinners to cook there tonight, so I'll see you later."

Jake left her to it, regretting that he'd said anything. He'd never met anyone quite so prickly. Even though they had been thrown together on and off for three days now, she didn't seem to be thawing in the slightest. Unlike the regulars in the bar at the hotel, who at least nodded at him when he walked through the door a few minutes later.

He saw the same faces he'd seen on his first night, and several more besides, and wondered if − like Wednesday's band night − this was the full village at play? Perhaps thirty people, tending towards the middle-aged and elderly − Jake was easily the youngest person there, as he took a seat at the bar.

No Duncan Fraser yet, but he'd be in at some point. The man basically lived in the place. You were guaranteed a sighting if you sat in the hotel long enough.

"Your usual, is it?" said Jimmy, suddenly looming, towering, and being generally enormous and frightening. "A pint of Berserker?"

"Erm, thanks but no, I think − "

"Haaaaa." Jimmy pointed a large, stubby finger at

Jake and laughed – or at least made a non-threatening gargling noise that Jake interpreted as a laugh. "Gotcha. One English beer coming up. You'll need about twelve of them, if you want a decent drink. And don't widdle on the carpet."

"Nice one, Jimmy," said someone in passing. Jake recognised one of the guitarists from Wednesday night. Whippet thin, an armful of tattoos, walked with the slightest of limps. The famous Ewan? The band member with a banged member.

Jake paid with one of the twenties Duncan had given him that morning and took a sip of his Little Widdle.

The good news was that if this became his usual drink, he'd never have to order it in person – say the mortifying words out loud. It would simply be supplied automatically when Jimmy saw him come in. That was something. Jake had never frequented a local pub where the host knew what his 'usual' was. The host here was terrifying, and Jake's new 'usual' tasted like warm dishwater that had been strained through a sweaty singlet, but you couldn't have everything.

Taking his cue from others at the bar, Jake summoned another pint by raising his finger, which – given Jimmy's usual demeanour – seemed like the most dangerously thrilling thing he'd ever done. Like a mouse flipping the bird at a lion.

And there he sat for an hour or so, a pint and a bit in, aching slightly from all the lifting and carrying he'd done, enjoying the hubbub of voices in the bar.

Thinking back over the last few days. Reckoning that he'd give it a few more at least. See if Duncan came up with any more money. And if not – well, it would have been a bit of a holiday, in a place that he never would have come otherwise. Though he had no idea what he'd do for the rest of the summer if he had to go home.

The main door from the harbourside opened – a bit more forcefully than usual – and a scruffy, bearded guy staggered in, already a bit the worse for wear. In his sixties, maybe, seventies even. Dressed in classic short-hand-for-farmer togs – baggy brown cords tucked into wellies, a beige jumper that was more stains than mate-rial, torn combat jacket that had battled a thousand barbed-wire fences, and a shapeless cap that could no longer strictly be said to be flat.

He ignored the room and slalomed his way to the bar, other end of the counter from Jake, waving a ten-pound note in front of him like a semaphore flag. Jimmy saw him and said something to one of his band mates, who looked over and groaned.

"Aye, aye," someone else shouted from inside the room, over the chatter. "Here he is, it's the Fairy King himself!"

"Bastards!" roared the man. "Whisky, Jimmy, come on, let's be having it."

Chapter 8

Jimmy poured the old guy a dram. Jake heard him say, "You all right? We going to be nice and quiet?" and the man grunted.

The background chatter returned to the bar, punctuated by an occasional louder laugh which seemed to be prompted by the new arrival. He knew it, too, if the way he kept twisting his neck around to see who was laughing was anything to go by. "Bastards," he mumbled every now and again, before throwing down the whisky and signalling for another.

Bangkok Ewan appeared at the bar, and shot a glance at the man.

"Seen any of the wee fellas today, eh, Ruan?" He smirked at Jimmy, who shook his head in warning.

"You'll see, you'll see," said the old guy.

"Leave him be," said Jimmy. "A nice, quiet drink, isn't that right, Ruan?"

"They're worth ten of you, you've no idea. My wee pals, you'll see."

Jimmy poured him another whisky and signalled for Bangkok to move away and wait for his drinks. The tattooed guitarist sidled down the bar, stood next to Jake and nodded a greeting.

"You're the English? One of the Crowthers, maybe?"

This again. What must it be like to be one of the Elsay Crowthers? Forever cursed by a bloodline of weak tea and warm beer. You'd never set foot outside your door.

"Jake." He offered his hand. "Not a Crowther, as far as I know."

"The English that got my job?"

Jake had had two pints and had mellowed out, so he wasn't as floored by this as he might have been, but he still spluttered and started apologising. Not for being English, though he figured that might have helped, but for stealing another man's job. Alva had warned him.

"Just kidding," said Bangkok, who introduced himself. As Ewan, not Bangkok. Right, noted.

"What's he paying you?" he said.

"A hundred. So far."

"So far!" Bangkok snorted heavily, like this was an excellent joke. "You'll learn. He'll have you doing all sorts. I only said two-fifty because I didn't want to do it. I know what Duncan Fraser's like. He'd buy someone's granny if he could, just so he could sell her at a profit."

Jimmy delivered a pint to Bangkok, who took the

top third off in one swallow. Jake saw a chance to change the subject.

"What's all that about?" he said, nodding towards the old man at the end of the bar.

"Oh, that's Ruan. Old Ruan Strang." Bangkok took another deep draught. Tapped his head. "Not quite right, up here," he said. "Reckons there's fairies in his glen." He raised his voice. "Isn't that right, Ruan? Wee fellas? Running about the place, bold as brass?"

"Bastard!" roared Strang, banging his whisky glass on the counter.

"Would you leave him alone," said Jimmy. "I'm not having all that again. Let him have his drink, and he'll be off."

Bangkok grumbled a bit, finished his pint, signalled for another, and went off to join his mates in the corner.

"Fairies?" said Jake, quizzically, then thought better of his tone. He didn't want to upset anyone else if he could help it. Who knew what folktales still lingered on in isolated communities like this? Hopefully, not *Midsommar*-style stories of sacrifice and slaughter, but fairy folk, little people? "I mean, I know that's a thing that some people believe in?" he said, covering himself. "Old stories, Celtic folklore, that sort of thing?"

"Aye," said Jimmy, resting his elbows on the counter, drawing Jake in. "Ancient lore, that's it. Handed down by the old folk, father to son, mother to daughter. They say, on a clear night, when the moon is high over the loch, and you see the dancing lights in the woods – "

"Yes?" said Jake.

"Bugger off," said Jimmy. "What are we, island bumpkins, dancing around bloody fairy rings? Is that what you think of us?" He drew himself up to his full height, which was considerable, and Jake realised that he had managed to offend without meaning to, all over again.

But Jimmy was also just kidding. He came back down to Jake's level and kept his voice down.

"Ruan, he lives in the old Strang place, the big house over the back of the island, the one with the closed road – maybe you've seen it?"

"I've seen the road. I didn't know there was a house beyond it."

"Aye, there is. Just the one. That was Ruan's parents' place – the Strang family goes way back, and Ruan's dad was a canny man, wealthy apparently, though you'd never know it. He was the one who built the hotel here, back in the 1950s." Jimmy slapped the counter in confirmation.

"Anyway, Ruan came back here with his wife when the old folks were ailing, and after they died – oh, twenty years ago now – the two of them stayed on. And then Ruan's wife, Eileen, died, five years ago, and the old lad has been there on his own since. Always liked a drink, but he got worse after Eileen died – bit more erratic, let himself go."

They both looked across at Ruan Strang, sunk into his whisky glass.

"And the fairies?" said Jake.

"It's just the drink talking," said Jimmy. "He's all right when he's sober. Not that he's sober much. He came in one day, three, four years back, shouting about fairies in the glen. His wee pals, all that. The lads here have never let him forget it. But to be honest, we don't see him much, except when he comes in here occasionally. He's no harm. I give him a few whiskies and hope no one riles him too much. He's a bit cracked but stronger than you think. Alva's the only one that can calm him down, if he gets lairy."

"Alva can?"

"Aye, she works there, up at the Strang place, three times a week, bit of cleaning and cooking. Doubt he could stay up there on his own, otherwise."

By Jake's reckoning, that made at least three jobs that Alva had. She seemed to be running the whole island. The only job she wasn't doing was cleaning out the rooms down at Castle View, though – as he was beginning to learn – being on Duncan Fraser's payroll wasn't any guarantee of actual wages.

"Drink!" roared Strang, suddenly, sparking into life. Which, in turn, brought a trilled rendition of, "I do believe in fairies, I do, I do!" from somewhere in the bar.

"Bastards!"

"Here we go," said Jimmy. "Never a dull moment."

"You lot, that's enough," said Alva, coming through from the kitchen, carrying plates, which she delivered to a table. "I've told you before, leave him alone."

She stood at the bar, close to the old man. "What are you doing here, Ruan?" she said, gently.

"Drink," he muttered.

"Why don't I run you home? Come on now." She helped him up from the bar stool. "You should have called me," she said to Jimmy.

"He was all right, till they started."

"They always start, you know that. Should be ashamed of yourselves." She addressed the room, and most had the good grace to look sheepish. "Keys," she snapped at Jimmy, who handed her the fob for his Land Rover.

"What'll we do about the dinners?"

"Should have thought of that, shouldn't you. Anyway, I'll be there and back, get him settled in, I won't be long. But he shouldn't be down here, you know what he's like."

"Maybe if you didn't do so much for him, he'd have sold up by now."

Alva turned and glared – full strength, stun-gun of a look.

"Yeah, well, that's not up to you, Jimmy Mac, is it now?" She put an arm around Ruan Strang's shoulder and helped him to the door.

Chapter 9

On the following Wednesday, Duncan asked Jake to help him pick up some more boxes from the afternoon ferry. Jake got the impression he didn't want Alva to find out, which was understandable. "Need to know, Jake," he said. "Need to know. Anyway, she's up at the Strang place today, so I could do with your help, all right?"

"OK, I suppose."

"Good man. Right, Alva's got the van, so you'll need to get the Land Rover off Jimmy," and with that, Duncan was gone, waving cheerily as he crunched down the gravel at Castle View.

There were two problems with this, as far as Jake was concerned.

One, Duncan, had never even asked him if he could drive. Technically, he could. He had passed his test the previous summer. But he had only ever driven with an instructor, until the test day itself. He hadn't driven since. And he certainly had never driven a Land Rover. So, there was that.

Two – *get the Land Rover off Jimmy*? Was he mad?

Jimmy had told Jake the story about Ruan Strang on the previous Saturday night, and that short conversation was the longest interaction that he had had with Jimmy in the week he'd been on the island. Apart from threatening drinks' references, that was the *only* thing Jimmy had said to him up until this point. Jake didn't think that made them bosom buddies yet. He couldn't imagine they were on Land-Rover-borrowing terms.

Then again, he supposed it was on a par with leaving your front door unlocked, using someone else's hotel kitchen, and sleeping in an abandoned activity centre. Maybe it was just how they did things on Elsay?

Jimmy, for his part, didn't seem surprised, though he did say, "Did he now?" when Jake told him Duncan had suggested it.

"You can take it," he said, handing over the keys outside the hotel. "Drive it down the ferry and back, no problem." He grasped Jake's hand without warning, and looked down at him, not breaking eye contact. "But if you prang it – "

He didn't specify what would happen, but the number of Rs and Gs he managed to get into the word 'prang' left Jake in little doubt about his meaning.

"Right, thanks," said Jake, disengaging his hand. "Understood."

Jimmy disappeared back inside, and Jake had a quick look at the vehicle before setting off, which reassured him somewhat. From the amount of dints and scrapes, there had clearly been some pre-pranging by other people – anything he could manage to do on a ten-mile round trip probably wouldn't even be noticed.

He crashed the gears a few times but reached the ferry without incident. The boxes were already on the quayside, labelled for D. Fraser but with no clue as to their contents. Gift shop stuff, no doubt. Far Eastern sweatshops working overtime again.

Jake loaded them up and turned back for Port Levin, window down, enjoying the sense of freedom. Coastal road, sun on his arm, a set of un-pranged wheels. Life was all right. You'd play driving music at this point – something loud and twentieth-century on Classic Rock FM, 'Radar Love,' maybe – if you weren't in a vehicle that had a hole in the dashboard where the CD player and radio used to be.

He slowed down at the Castle View driveway, preparing for the turn, but realised Duncan hadn't said where he wanted the boxes. If they were for the shop, there was no point taking them to Castle View. The hotel then – take the Land Rover back and drop the boxes, two birds with one stone. It's not like Duncan was ever anywhere else, anyway.

And he would have done exactly that, except that instead Jake found himself turning up the minor road shy of the village – the one he'd walked up before. The road to the head of the loch, and – he now knew – to the Strang house.

Since that first day, he'd had another look at the map on the activity centre wall. Jimmy had said it was a closed road, and there was certainly a gate across it, he already knew that. But the map clearly showed it was a public road – a 'Byway Open to All Traffic,' it was known as apparently, when Jake had traced the route with his finger and looked up the definition on the map key. It wasn't supposed to be closed or have a gate across it. You were allowed to drive a vehicle along there.

The road led through a glen and down to the loch and a beach. And on a fine summer's day, and in temporary possession of a Land Rover, why not have another attempt at reaching there? See if he could get through the gate. Have a paddle in the water, maybe? What was the harm?

He recalled what Jimmy had said about Alva going up there a couple of times a week – and she had borrowed the Land Rover herself on Saturday night to drive Ruan Strang home. Plus, Duncan had mentioned that she had taken the van up to Strang's house today.

So, call him Sherlock, that meant the road was entirely driveable. And he had an off-road vehicle, in any case. Not that Jake intended to go even an inch off-road, because that could only lead to pranging. And pranging would result in a difficult conversation with a shaven-headed folk-punk landlord, and no one wanted that.

The first part of the road was fine. A bit narrow

maybe, but it was unlikely he was going to meet anything coming the other way. And it would only be Alva, anyway. Unless – sudden thought – it was a massive prancing deer, bounding out of the trees, so that caused him to take his foot off the gas a bit.

It soon became more track-like and Jake had to concentrate, as he dropped the Land Rover into second gear and navigated the potholes and rougher sections. And all that took him about five minutes until the gate came into view again, whereupon he stopped a few feet short and got out.

He remembered the gate had a chain, which he hadn't examined before, and when he did now, he discovered it was padlocked shut. Which was annoying, and illegal, or contrary to the Highway Code, or something. But either way, he wasn't going to be able to drive the Land Rover any further. Although he did wonder how Alva had got through?

He stood at the gate for a minute or two, pondering. Maybe he could leave the vehicle and hop over, walk up to the loch? The passive-aggressive 'Keep Out' signs and warning notices were all still in place, but now that Jake had seen Ruan Strang in person, he didn't think he had much cause for concern.

True, it was a bit Blair-Witchy here in the trees, and the old man was decidedly odd, if not off his rocker. But he was a drinker, and being drunk, and odd, and shouting about fairies, wasn't the same as being dangerous. In any case, he'd surely be up at the house with

Alva today? Strang would never even see him jump the gate.

Reluctantly, however, Jake decided that he better not leave the Land Rover in the road. Just his luck if someone else did come up, or Alva came back. He'd never hear the end of that. He'd come back another day, on foot, and persevere this time.

There wasn't a lot of room to turn the Land Rover around. Jake had a look on both sides of the track, where crowding trees left a scarce few feet to operate in. That made him feel momentarily sick with nerves, but he did remember his driving instructor saying that, when turning a car around, the number of turns didn't matter. It was doing it safely and under control that was the important thing. Which meant it was time for an extremely careful twenty-seven-point turn.

As he was about to open the door and climb in, a movement in the trees caught his eye. Over the gate and in the woods, a hundred feet away, between two trunks close to the track. Bloody deer? He clapped his hands to see if he could make it move again.

Nothing stirred for a few seconds, until – there it was again. Not a deer. An obvious figure this time, closing in on the next tree, shortening the distance to the gate.

The figure stepped out. Even under dappled light in the woods, Jake could see the shotgun cradled in the crook of an arm – and the green, brown and beige ensemble of a scruffy farmer.

"Bastard!" yelled Ruan Strang, advancing. "Leave my wee pals alone!"

Jake watched the man reach into a jacket pocket, bring his hand across to the barrels, close and raise the shotgun – and then, incredibly, as far as Jake was concerned, fire into the air.

The noise echoed through the trees, lifting screeching birds into the sky, and Jake hunched his shoulders and flinched.

Said, "Fuck me," a few times, rapidly.

Grabbed at the door handle, dived in, started the engine, lurched forward and stalled because it had been in gear, said "Fuck's SAKE!" and tried again.

Strang had made up more ground and was waving the shotgun around – Jake could see him through the windscreen – none of which was conducive to a calm and controlled twenty-seven-point turn.

Jake did his best, grinding through reverse and first, and managed to turn the Land Rover in the road. He had no idea how, and heard a scrape or two, but that was the least of his worries at this point. He'd have failed his test, for sure, but you know what – out of here, *sayonara.*

As he made the final turn and straightened up, he could see in the rear-view mirror that Strang had reached the gate and was resting his shotgun on the top. He was still shouting and gesticulating with one fist, and as Jake roared off – scattering dirt and pebbles – there was another loud report.

Jake put his foot down, the engine roaring, the Land

Rover careering down the road, but he still heard the metallic patter at the back of the vehicle.

"Fuck me," he said one final time, as the track turned to tarmac and the junction came back into view.

Jimmy hadn't defined terms exactly, but Jake suspected that having the Land Rover peppered with shot by a mad old sod would count as a pranging.

Chapter 10

Duncan was of the same mind as Jake.

"Bloody hell," he said, inspecting the back of the Land Rover. "Ruan Strang? Are you sure?"

Jake had driven straight back to Castle View, heart pounding, hoping to find a quiet, private place to hyperventilate, swear a lot more, and possibly have a cardiac arrest. Instead, Duncan had been there, poking around in the skip at the front.

"Am I sure that someone pointed a shotgun at me and fired at the Land Rover? Pretty sure." His hands were still shaking.

"He's getting worse," said Duncan. "I've told Alva, but she doesn't listen."

"Was she there, up at the house, do you reckon?"

"Ah, no, she's long back. She's over at the hotel, I've just come from there."

"What does she go up there for, anyway?"

"Bit of housekeeping, this and that. Runs him up

some provisions from the ferry most weeks. Does some cooking and cleaning. Says he's harmless, but needs a bit of help around the place."

"Harmless?"

"Mostly, until now. You don't see him much. When you do, it's usually the shouting and drinking. The shooting's new. I'll have to tell Alva."

Duncan bent down and had another look at the back of the vehicle. Sucked his breath in through his teeth, like a mechanic just about to fleece you for a replacement part that you've never even heard of. New flux capacitor, mate, that's going to cost you.

"Jimmy won't be happy," he said.

Jake's stomach gave another lurch, realising that his day wasn't going to get any better. He still had to tell the thrash-metal licensee the bad news.

Duncan, meanwhile, was looking in the back, checking over his boxes.

"They seem all right," he said. "Could have been worse. Very delicate, those Saharan glass wind-chimes. What were you doing up there anyway?"

Jake didn't like the way this was slowly becoming all his own fault. "Thought I'd drive around to the loch," he said. "Nice day and all that. It's a public road, or at least it should be. It shouldn't have a gate across it!"

"Oh, yeah, the gate. Someone should have said."

"You think?"

Duncan patted his boxes and closed the Land Rover door.

"See, Alva's got a key. She's the only one who goes up there now, lets herself through when she needs to."

"But it's a public road? Says so on the map."

"Well, yes – bit of a sore point on the island, to tell the truth. It is, but the land on either side is Ruan Strang's, including the bay at the head of the loch. And the road doesn't go anywhere else, only to the Strang house and the loch. Historically, there was always access to the cliffs, coves and woods around there – that's where we did all our kayaking, abseiling, wood-craft and beachcombing. Drove the families up from the Centre here. We paid Strang a retainer every year to use his land, all hunky dory."

"And then?"

"Well, there's the thing. Strang's wife, Eileen died, and he went a bit off the rails, until about a year or so later, he withdrew permission to use his land. That was four years ago now. For a while, we tried to run the activities down in the south of the island instead – the other way from the ferry port – but it's nowhere near as convenient, and it's a whole lot windier, more exposed. The families didn't like it, we got some bad reviews. And – well, that's where we are."

"Strang closed down your business?"

"Not just him. Let's say he didn't help. But the man was grieving, and it is his land."

"Doesn't explain the road, though? Why it's closed?"

"Like I said, the road doesn't go anywhere else. He put the gate and the fencing up a while back, made it clear he didn't want anyone on his land. The village has mostly let him be, though there's a few that are pissed off with him. It's why they give him the needle, about the fairies and that."

"What, they want access to that end of the loch? To go to the beach?"

"Ah, well, you wouldn't know, would you? No, not that. Ruan Strang had an offer last year to buy the house and all the land. I say house. It's a big, old mansion, got its own beach and jetty, woodland, you name it. The estate agent over from the mainland reckoned it was for a hotel chain, after a location for a luxury, hideaway resort. Would have transformed the island. We're struggling here, you've seen. This would have meant jobs, money, a future. Maybe I'd have been able to fold the Centre into it, too – you know, become their activity provider?"

"And Strang turned it down?"

"Wouldn't even talk to them. Had Alva tell them no. She didn't make any friends over that, I can tell you."

Jake wondered if this went some way towards accounting for Alva's demeanour. She wasn't exactly friendly to anyone, but if she'd been copping flak for this, that might explain it?

"She did that? She turned down the offer for Strang?"

Duncan scratched his head, like it was still a bit of a mystery to him.

"She's been working for him for a couple of years,

since she – well, anyway. Seems to like him. Maybe feels a bit responsible for him. I don't get it myself, but she's made it pretty clear to everyone. If Strang doesn't want to sell, she's not going to try and persuade him. He's lived there twenty-odd years, his family for sixty before that. Just looking out for him, I suppose."

"That's awkward."

"Not for me. Look, everyone knows what Alva's like. You've met her. If she doesn't want to do something, you'll not change her mind. I like that about her, if I'm honest. Stands up for what she believes in."

"Even so, it must be difficult for her?" Jake had been brushed off when he'd tried, clumsily, to ask Alva why she still lived on the island. What he'd heard seemed to give her even more reasons to leave. "She's happy here, doing odd jobs and the like?"

"It's her home, Jake. Maybe it's different down south, I don't know. But when you come from a place like this, it gets in your bones. She did leave, as it happens – went to uni in Edinburgh, came back at the end of her first year for the summer, and never went back. Two years ago now. Interruption of studies, they call it. For anxiety. Mental-health break. I don't know, she won't really talk to me about it. Says she'll go back when she's good and ready, but she's still here. She keeps herself busy – the hotel, the shop, the Strang place. And I like having her around – when she's not giving me a hard time, that is."

Duncan winked at Jake, who considered all this new information.

Alva had talked about commitments, as a reason not to leave. But she *had* left once, albeit briefly, and had then come home again. And Jake knew of at least two or three people in his year in London who had taken a break from their studies for similar reasons as her, so that made some sense.

There was even that guy, Jed, was it, who had gone interrailing last summer and never came back to college? Just disappeared without trace. You never knew what was going on in other people's lives. What problems they might have. What choices they might have to make.

Alva had also seemed to suggest that looking out for Duncan was at least part of the reason for her to stay. And she did give her dad a hard time, no question. Because he was a chancer? An amiable chancer – there was no real malice in him, as far as Jake could see – but Alva probably felt someone had to keep an eye on his various schemes and ruses.

Duncan, true to form, reverted to type, as he examined the Land Rover one final time.

"Tell you what," he said. "I'll scrape some gravel over those marks. I don't think it caught much of a blast. You stay here, do a bit more in the house. I'll run the Land Rover up to the hotel, tell Jimmy it was me driving, if he even notices. Say I backed it into the wall here."

"Really?" Jake felt a wave of relief. "You'd do that? Won't he have a go at you?"

"Well, look, if he does, I'll take it out of your wages,

for emotional distress. You do another day here tomorrow and we'll call it even?"

"Wages? What wages? Hang on," said Jake, but Duncan was already revving the engine.

Chapter 11

Jake went up to the hotel later that Wednesday evening for band night – Jimmy, Bangkok Ewan and his mate on duelling guitars, and the twin fiddle players, appearing this week as Eighties' covers band, Phoney M. Good name, to be fair.

Jake kept out of Jimmy's way as much as he could, but either he hadn't noticed the pranging or Fraser had copped the blame. Nothing was said, in any case, and Jake stayed for the undeniably novel experience that was a bullet-headed landlord in a white suit leading a mass Rickroll singalong and flash-mob dance for 'Never Gonna Give You Up.'

Jake managed to sit that one out at the bar, but old Mrs Dunmore from the village shop grabbed his wrist during the first chorus of 'I Should Be So Lucky.' "Tally ho! English," she said, and hauled him off his barstool. She'd been busting moves since he first came in, and had worked her way through most of the regulars, so Jake supposed that counted as another kind of acceptance.

"I don't really dance," he said.

"Nonsense, dearie," she said. "Of course you do, look!" and she swirled him around with a surprisingly strong grip. "It's not proper music, mind, but it will have to do. If you're still here in a couple of weeks when the laddies do the thrash-metal, we'll do the moshing together, how does that sound?"

Jake laughed – truthfully, that sounded awesome – and Mrs Dunmore spun him around one more time, before careering across the room to find another victim. Yet another entry in the 'You couldn't make it up' ledger. Yes, his mates were going to *American Pie*-style toga parties with ripped fitness instructors, but he was on a promise to do the Hammer of Thor with a Scottish septuagenarian shopkeeper.

He had another drink or two, scanning the room, but didn't see Alva to talk to. And at the end of the night, Duncan was elusive when Jake tried to pin him down about getting paid for his work.

"Might have a little something for you next week," Duncan said. "Let's see how the shop goes on Saturday?" Which was not encouraging, seeing as how poorly the sales had gone the previous week. And nor was, "You'll not mind giving Alva a hand again, will you?"

It was pretty much as Alva, Bangkok Ewan, and almost anyone else who knew him had suggested to Jake over the last week – Duncan Fraser was full of it.

And Jake was running out of money. After buying drinks and food, he had fifty quid of Fraser's hundred left, and another emergency hundred hidden in his bag at Castle View.

It was the middle of June. He'd expected to have been earning money by now. His college fund was on the low side, and the next student loan payment wouldn't kick in until the autumn.

Basically, he had no choice. If there wasn't any paying work here, he'd have to go back. To the English seaside, café drudgery, overbearing parents, annoying customers, and to the many, many murders he'd be forced to commit between now and the start of the new term.

He did still have free accommodation and meals here, though, so Jake decided to stick it out until the following week and call Duncan's bluff. If there was nothing for him by Monday or Tuesday – actual cash in hand, not a promise – he'd be on the midweek ferry.

Meanwhile, Duncan could go whistle. Jake had put in five full days of work since he'd been on the island, both in the Castle View house and the gift shop, plus all the fetching and carrying. Forty hours for a hundred quid was two pounds fifty an hour, which was a joke.

No, two could play at that game. Jake was downing tools.

He spent a day pottering around the harbour, and climbing up to the castle ruins. He sat up there for a while in the sun, looking across the water – the mainland, a long way away, obscured by a shimmering mist.

It was undeniably attractive – more ruggedly beautiful than pretty – but he couldn't imagine living here. Not that he was a city boy, particularly, but Elsay felt too remote – too end-of-the-line – to be a place he could settle. One road, one shop, one pub – you'd need a very good reason to make this your home.

On the Friday, he walked the five miles from the village down to the ferry port and continued along a wide but rough track, which curled west and then north a little way, before petering out at a turning circle.

It was as Duncan had said. There were a couple of stony beaches, and a rocky promontory or two, but the sea was rougher on this side and the wind whipped across his face. Not a scrap of shelter anywhere, and not exactly conducive to hosting jolly family activities – just an exposed coastline and a vast expanse of churning water beyond.

Keep going west and the next land you reached was Newfoundland, two thousand miles away. Where there was probably another remote settlement with one road, one shop and one pub. He waved across the ocean at whichever poor soul had ventured all the way there for a summer job, and hoped they were having better luck than him.

Jake debated going to help at the shop on Saturday, as Duncan had asked, but he was enjoying exploring the island. Added to which, there was the matter of Alva herself. Given that it was never difficult to distinguish between a snippy Emma Stone-lookalike with a grievance and a ray of sunshine, he rather thought he'd give it a miss.

She had to be there, it was her dad's shop, but he didn't. Not until he got paid, anyway.

He found himself coming back to the idea of Ruan Strang's bay at the head of the loch. There were some pictures in one of the brochures left lying around in the staff quarters, and he could see how losing access to it must have hit Duncan hard.

It was stunning – a stubby inlet with green-topped cliffs on either side, a crescent of white sand at its head, a wooded glen behind, and a single-track road leading up into the trees. An aerial shot in the brochure showed tiny coves to the north, beyond the loch, with rocky outcrops, turquoise waters and more white sand.

Jake had had no idea Scotland could look like this. If this was to be his last weekend, he had to see it, but he wasn't going to try the road again. Shot at once was more than enough. He didn't know if anyone had had words with Strang, or even if it would make a difference if they had, but on reflection he'd leave the approach by road well alone.

However, he might be able to climb the cliffs above the harbour and see if he could get a view from the top somewhere? He'd like to see it, that's all, and the map at Castle View showed a track or two winding up from the quayside in the village. They dwindled into nothing higher up, but Jake had noticed the odd sheep grazing up there – white against the patches of green and brown – and figured he could tramp in their tracks until he could see down the other side to the loch.

It's not as if doddery Strang was going to be wandering around up there like Heathcliff over the heather. If the photos were anything to go by, the house was way out of sight, at the top of the glen. And if Strang was down by the water for any reason, he'd hardly notice Jake – who, in any case, would be well out of shotgun range.

He slipped through the village on Saturday afternoon, avoiding the harbour front and the shop, in case Alva or Duncan spotted him. A handful of cyclists milled around on the quayside, having ridden up from the ferry, and were eating sandwiches and dangling their legs over the harbour wall. Another run on Eiffel Towers and Albanian socks was on the cards.

He found a flight of concrete steps around the back of the hotel, which soon turned into a rougher track. There was a bench twenty feet up which gave a nice view of the harbour and village, and then a scramble behind that led onto a zig-zag path through the heather.

At some point that stopped too, and the heather stretched on before him, rising gently, with cliffs, sea and harbour over to the righthand side. Jake kept going, picking his way through the less dense patches, trying to remember if it was Scotland or Ireland that didn't have any snakes. An occasional sheep scurried out of the way, and something – a bird? – shot out of the heather as he tramped past.

And, suddenly, there it was.

He was on the brow of a hill, with a sweeping view down into the loch, with Strang's bay at the far end. He was seeing it from a different vantage point from the photos, but it was recognisably the same place – a steep-sided inlet ending in a perfect arc of white sand, with a wooden pier leading out into the water and a small, clapboard building at the end of it. A boathouse?

On the other side of the inlet, cliffs rose again – higher and more sheer than on this side – while a dense wedge of green spread inland from the beach. That must be the glen and – under the trees, not visible from here – was the minor road up to the house, which carried on all the way around through the woods to the gate. The side from which Strang had been waving his gun around.

No sign of him, at least. Just the peace and quiet of a Scottish island summer, a hidden sweep of sand, and distant ripples on the water.

Jake took a panoramic snap on his phone, and then picked up a sheep track that took him over the brow before descending gently at an angle, down the near side of the inlet. He thought he'd go a little further before turning back – grab some better photos at least.

In another few minutes, the track had brought him down a fair distance, twisting this way and that, under overhanging gorse bushes. He looked up behind him and could no longer see the top of the cliff on his side.

As he descended closer to the water line, there were glimpses of the inlet away to his right through gaps in the bushes. The heather flattened out in front of him, and then – just like that – he was on a grassy bluff, twenty feet above the beach. A scramble down some rocks and he'd be there.

That was quick. He hadn't expected to come this far, and he paused for a long moment, taking a few more pictures.

It was quiet and deserted – only the sound of the water and the distant peep-peep of a bird on the hill behind him. The sand was Caribbean white, and the water an inviting blue, though he knew from dipping his hand in the Port Levin harbour that it would be freezing. There was a line of bladderwrack seaweed halfway up the beach, and a couple of bleached tree branches washed up against the boulders below.

It was perfect. And there was no one around.

No way to get here either, unless you were Strang, and Jake would see him coming easily – out of the glen, a few hundred yards away, and onto the beach. Jake reckoned he could be back up the rocks and away up the hillside before Strang would even spot him.

Jake sat there for a few more minutes, crouching and watching, waiting to see if anything changed, but it really was like a desert island down there. Completely silent and secluded.

He made his mind up. Down onto the beach, dip his feet in the water to say he'd been, and quickly away. No one would ever know he'd trespassed.

Jake stepped off the grass and onto the rocks and picked his way carefully down. There were big slabs, where the cliff had subsided in the past, and then a jumble of smaller rocks that formed a scree.

Five or six feet from the bottom – three or four steps away from the sand – his front foot gave way under a sliding rock, and he fell forwards and down.

He put an arm out and broke his fall, but that just tumbled him over, and he rolled the last few feet, flailing. He hit the sand hard, and his head harder, on a stone that was partly covered, and passed out.

When he opened his eyes, groaning – a few minutes later, an hour, Jake didn't know – it was because he could feel something on his chest, and something else poking him in the side. And there was a shadow across the top half of his body.

The thing on his chest was a foot-high fairy. The thing poking him was another foot-high fairy with a stick. And the shadow was Ruan Strang, standing over him with a shotgun.

"That's him, General," said Strang. "The wee bastard."

Chapter 12

Jake must have passed out more than once because –
later – nothing that he did remember made much
sense.

He had been sick on the beach, he remembered
that. Or perhaps not sick? He had hazy memories of
spitting out sand from his mouth, from where his head
had lolled sideways. He'd felt dizzy when he moved.
Nauseous. Dry mouth. Did that mean he was
concussed?

He'd also felt a rolling motion, like he was on a
boat. But he didn't remember walking. Had he been
carried somewhere? Transported? He didn't know.

A face had loomed over him – whiskers, a beard.
Ruan Strang? Certainly, the word 'Bastard' came and
went, somewhere in the background.

Strang's beach, that was it. That's where he had
been. He had been coming down the hillside. He'd seen

the view and had wanted to take a closer look. And then what?

At one point, he'd found himself lying flat on his back on tarmac. He remembered the feel of the surface underneath his splayed fingers. No longer the beach. A road? He had tried to raise himself on his elbows but felt a downward pressure and then more motion. More nausea.

When he was next conscious of his surroundings, he was in a room. Light coming in through a window. Sitting on the floor, his back against the side of a double bed. A bedroom. Not his bedroom – not the bunk-room at the Castle View. Somewhere else. Strang's house? Jake couldn't make sense of any of it. How the hell had he got here?

The bedroom door was open, but all he could see of the room beyond was an oval dining table. The edge of a dark green sofa with carved wooden legs. A cabinet full of glassware.

His head throbbed and his mouth was parched.

"I don't know," said Strang, from somewhere in the other room, out of sight. "Sneaky beggar. I wouldn't be surprised."

There was the sound of pacing footsteps. "Aye," he heard Strang say. "Good idea. I'll ask."

Jake felt the back of his head and winced. A huge bump. He no longer felt sick, but he had a mighty headache and there was sand down the back of his neck. He wondered about trying to get to his feet, and drew his knees towards himself. One ankle was sore, where he'd turned it as he fell.

That was it. He'd fallen. Off the rocks, onto the beach. Hit his head. And then something else – ?

There was a sound from the adjacent room. A fluttering, and then bumps or thumps.

Strang spoke again. "Yessir, you can count on me," he said. "No one will find out."

There was silence, and then Jake heard footsteps and the sound of a door closing somewhere else in the house.

He struggled to his feet and sat on the edge of the bed, by which time the footsteps were back. Strang put his head round the door, saw that Jake was starting to rise, and said, "Oh, no you don't. No, no, no."

He stepped back and closed the door, and Jake heard a key turn in the lock.

"You'll keep, *sassenach*," he heard Strang say. "Orders is orders."

Jake tried the door and called out, but Strang's footsteps retreated. He rattled the handle and shouted this time, which elicited a roar of "Bastard!" from Strang.

Jake felt in his pocket for his phone. Not there. He couldn't remember if he had had it with him or not. Had it fallen out on the sand? It must have done.

He sat back on the bed and closed his eyes. Just for a moment.

When he woke again, it was still light outside, but this time of year that could have meant it was five pm or ten pm. Still Saturday? Was it the evening? The shadows suggested it was. There were loud sounds coming from the other room – bangs and curses, the scrape of a chair, the chink of a glass against a bottle.

"Not my wee pals!" Strang was shouting. "I won't have it!"

Jake rattled the door one more time and shouted to be let out.

"Mine!" roared Strang. "They came to me! Not you!"

There was a window looking out on a small court-yard, with a couple of faded, plastic garden chairs and a planter filled with weeds. Jake tried to lift the sash but there were window locks on either side; it raised maybe an inch and no more. He wasn't getting out that way. Unless he broke the glass? It might come to that.

"Strang? Ruan?" said Jake. "Open the door." He had meant to sound commanding, but he could hear the weakness in his own voice. This was very far from being a good situation – and no one knew he was here.

The mad old sod had already unloaded a shotgun at him. Jake didn't want to rile him any further, but equally, he didn't want to be locked in a lunatic's bedroom in a remote house. Or embark on a sequence of events that would lead inexorably to him being buried alive in the woods or skinned to make a face mask. There were any number of films that suggested that that was next on the agenda. None, that he could recall, set on a Scottish island, but there was always a first time for everything.

He shook the door one more time, hoping it might spring open but knowing it wouldn't.

"Quiet! That's enough from you now." Jake heard the TV go on and the volume was raised. Over booming dialogue there was an occasional shout from Strang and, in quieter moments, the clink and gurgle of another drink being poured. A glass broke. Another roar from Strang.

Drinking noises, though. Not, say, blade-sharpening noises or the whine of a wood-chipper. That was something.

As the drink apparently flowed next door, Jake gave up trying to attract Strang's attention. He lay down and eventually he slept, the TV invading his dreams – of faces and beards and sand and a wild, whisky-soaked jailer. At some point, when it was darker, the TV went off, and there was one last crash of glass, and then silence.

Jake awoke to different sounds and knew from the light in the room that it was morning. Sunday morning. He'd been here – what? Fifteen, eighteen hours? No one would have missed him.

He could hear glass being swept up in the other room, and a vacuum cleaner being run. There were heavy sighs, and the sound of furniture being moved around.

A door opened somewhere. An indistinct voice. An answer, a muffled conversation. Footsteps across the room. The key turned in the lock.

"I had no choice," said Strang, opening the door. "He saw them."

"Oh, Ruan," said Alva, looking at Jake, on the bed. "What have you done?"

Chapter 13

Alva sat Jake down on the sofa, and brought him a jug of water, a cup of tea and a bacon sandwich. Like he'd come for breakfast.

Looked at the top of his head, peered into his eyes, did the follow-my-finger thing, declared him all right, but gave him two paracetamols anyway. First aid, delivered. Bedside manner, not great.

The room was full of old, oak furniture that looked solid and expensive. There were some large oil paintings on the walls – island landscapes – and a big rug with red, purple and green geometric shapes. One corner of it was turned over – Alva had been sweeping up glass shards from the floor.

Strang stood on the other side of the room, swaying a bit, eyes fixed on Jake, while Alva poured him another glass of water.

"Ruan says you fell?" she said. "Banged your head?"

All true, but that wasn't where Jake felt like starting the conversation. There was *way* more stuff that had happened since then that he felt like talking about. But Alva's presence had thrown him, so he began with his usual, favourite question.

"You?" he said. "What are you doing here?"

"I work here," said Alva. And when Jake looked puzzled, said, "You're at Ruan's house."

One mystery out of the way, though he'd guessed as much.

"More to the point," said Alva, "What are you doing here? You were supposed to be at the shop yesterday, helping me? You never turned up."

The shop. Jake had forgotten that he was supposed to have been there. So he had been missed, after all? Although apparently not enough for someone to have come looking for him.

"I went exploring," he said. "Over the cliffs."

"Dangerous," said Alva. "Could have told you that. Ruan found you on his beach. Brought you back here last night."

Not for the first time on this island, Jake felt like something was being made all his fault.

"He locked me in," he said. "You saw that. What's wrong with him?"

Strang bristled a bit but said nothing.

"He was worried about you, that's all. Didn't want you wandering off, what with the bang on your head. Thought it was safest."

Yeah, sure. *That* was the reason. Jake didn't have

the clearest of memories of the previous evening, but he hadn't been secured in a room for his own safety by a saintly Ruan Nightingale. Incarcerated for unknown reasons by Nurse Ratched in wellies and a tatty sweater, yes.

"There was something on the beach," said Jake. "I can't explain it. Two – creatures." Maybe more – Jake had hazy memories of others, by his side when he was on the ground. "Little," he said, holding his hands apart to show her. "And wings. They had wings." And as he said it, and realised how it sounded, he also knew it was true.

Alva laughed. "Wings?" she said. "Well, you *did* hit your head pretty hard. You've quite the bump."

Jake looked from Alva to Strang. The old man was grimacing and tapping one foot repeatedly on the floor. Jake could still smell the whisky – from Strang, or from wherever he had spilled it last night.

"I know what I saw," said Jake.

"Maybe you're concussed? Nearest doctor is on the mainland. I can get someone to run you over in a boat. Perhaps that's the best thing? Get you off the island, seen to properly?" She seemed energised by the suggestion.

Off the island? He'd only banged his head. It hardly required an emergency evacuation. There was something worrying her, though.

"I saw two things, creatures. He was with them." Jake pointed at Strang. "He was talking to them, I heard him. Then he locked me in there."

"Talking to creatures? Really? Nasty bump like that," said Alva. "Enough to scramble your brains, eh, Ruan?"

Strang looked miserable but nodded.

"And there's no way *he* got me here. Not on his own. Look at him. He can hardly stand up."

"That's because he's been drinking again," said Alva. "Which I've told him about," and she shot the old man a stern look.

"It wasn't my fault, Alva. The wee fellas needed a little stretch, you know?"

"Ruan!"

"They like it on the beach. Do their exercises and that – "

"Ruan!" Alva crossed the room and grasped Strang's hands. "That's enough!" She glanced over in Jake's direction.

"Yes, right, got you." Strang seemed to collect himself and then ruined it by tapping his nose, nodding sagely and winking at her.

"Anyone mind telling me what's going on?"

"Nothing," said Alva, forcefully.

"That's right," said Strang. "The wee fellas were never here." He tapped his nose again and poured himself a drink from a cabinet. "Never here," he repeated.

"Jesus," said Alva.

Jake looked at the pair of them again.

"Wee fellas?"

"Never here," mumbled Strang, now on his second

whisky of the morning. "You didn't see any of my wee pals, I remember now."

"Would you like to tell me?" Jake asked Alva. "Because this is getting weirder by the minute."

She looked across at him, calculating. "I can't," she said, finally.

"A secret," agreed Strang, grabbing the bottle and settling back on the sofa with Jake. "Can't tell anyone about the wee fellas, isn't that right, Alva?" He sat upright and brandished the bottle. "Because they were never here! Under the – you know, in their wee, erm – "

"Ruan, for God's sake!" She took the bottle from him. "How many times have I told you about the drinking?"

The old man's face fell. "Ah, it's lonely, Alva, you don't know. They're the only pals I have."

"That's not true, Ruan. And I do know how it is."

Jake had had enough. He still had a headache, had slept in his clothes, lost his phone, and had sand in his hair. Fair play, he'd had a bacon sandwich, but that hardly made up for it.

"I'm off," he said. "That mad old git shot at me yesterday, and kept me prisoner in here last night. And I'm beginning to think you're as barmy as he is. Something is definitely going on. Maybe I'll just ask Duncan?"

"You can't do that." A look fell across Alva's face that Jake couldn't read.

"Fraser!" roared Strang. "He'll not get his hands on them! Alva!"

"I know, Ruan, I know. But we've got a problem now, haven't we?" and she nodded at Jake.

"Don't worry, I'll fetch the shotgun!" Strang staggered to his feet. "Soon sort it out."

"What?"

"No one is getting a shotgun," said Alva. "For god's sake."

"No, right, the noise," said Strang. "A shovel, then? I've got one in the barn."

"Ruan, sit down and shut up. Let me think."

"So, just to be clear," said Jake. "We're ruling out the shotgun and the shovel? You're both deranged. And I'm leaving."

"Wait," said Alva. "Please." Her voice was flat, resigned. She looked at Strang and then back to Jake, having seemingly made up her mind.

"You can't tell," she said. "You can never tell. Not Duncan. Not anyone."

Chapter 14

Strang had quietened down and was slumbering at the end of the sofa, half snoring.

"He lived here with his wife, Eileen," said Alva. "Until she died."

"I heard."

"Five years ago now. He keeps it the same. So he can still picture her living here."

Jake looked around the room. He saw the family photographs on the mantelpiece for the first time. A bookcase full of old books with embossed lettering. A half-completed jigsaw on an occasional table. A decidedly un-smart TV on a teak table with a row of DVDs underneath. On second look, not even DVDs, videos. Your standard old-person living arrangement.

"They kept themselves to themselves, even back in the day. I was a young girl when they came to live here, but the family had been here for ever. Then, when Eileen died, Ruan became even more of a recluse."

"What's this got to do with anything?"

"It's so you understand what it means."

"I don't understand any of it," said Jake. "The wee fellas? His little pals?"

Strang stirred a little at this, before sinking back into the sofa.

"Ruan calls them fairies," said Alva. "According to him, they turned up one night a few years ago. On the beach down there, where he found you."

"Fairies?" Jake tried to keep his voice neutral. "Seriously?"

"That's what Ruan calls them, amongst other things. You've heard him. It's hard to get the full story, but it seems he went down to the beach one day for a walk, and there they were."

"They, being – ?"

"Sounds like you've seen them, too. You tell me."

Jake thought back, and tried to distinguish between head trauma and fact, dream and reality.

"About yea high," he said, holding one hand a foot off the floor. "Wings. Beards?"

"That's them," said Alva. "The fairies. Ruan's wee pals." She paused and then said, "Mine, too."

"But – "

"Yep."

'I mean – "

"I know."

"There's no such thing. They don't exist," said Jake automatically, realising that he wasn't so sure about that now.

"Try telling them that. They very much exist. And Ruan – here on his own in the house, after Eileen died – kept them a secret for a year or two. Well, not exactly a secret. Every time he had a drink and came into the village, he'd tell everyone. You saw him in the hotel the other night? Only, of course, no one believed him. They still don't. He's just old Ruan, on a bender, sad about his wife, poor old lad."

"But you've seen them?"

"Not at first. I didn't believe it either, I thought he was a crazy old man, like the others. Duncan used to tell me how he'd come in the hotel and start spouting off about his wee pals. I felt sorry for him, if anything. I always liked Eileen, she was kind to me. Used to play with me on the beach, and when I was older we'd sit out in the evening and look at the stars. And then I went away to uni."

"Your dad said."

"Did he now? What exactly did Duncan say?"

"Nothing really. Just that you were at college in Edinburgh. Used to be at college, anyway."

"Aye," said Alva. "Turns out that I was clever enough to go, after all."

She wasn't going to let that go then. Jake, wisely, said nothing.

"Came back for the summer holidays, a couple of years ago," she said. 'To work in his stupid shop. Help out at the activity centre – it was still a going concern, but on its last legs. He – Ruan – came in the hotel one night, and they were all going on at him. You can imagine. I thought they were being mean and that it wasn't fair, because he was obviously a bit, you know – not right in the head, something like that. So I put him in the van and said I'd take him home."

"And that's when you saw them?"

"Hard to miss. I got him through the door, and the TV was on. They were perched on the sofa watching it."

Jake wasn't sure he had heard correctly.

"They were watching TV? Fairies?"

"Strictly speaking, they were practising their English. But yes."

"This sofa?" Jake was still trying to process it all.

"Ruan kept saying, 'I told you!' and 'They'll see!' And then he passed out in his bedroom. And I was left here with them. They were watching that old TV version of *Pride and Prejudice*, and they weren't happy at being interrupted, Mr Darcy had just got out of the lake."

Jake laughed in disbelief. "This is mad. It can't be true."

"Depends on your definition of truth, I suppose."

"True, real, supported by facts! I mean, come on, fairies?"

"Oh, they're real, I assure you. And if they're not, what is it that you think you saw? Down on the beach there?"

Jake had no answer to that.

"And 'fairies' is just what Ruan calls them. It's the wings. You can see why he latched onto that."

"They can fly?"

"More like a power-assisted hover, I suppose. I don't think they can go very high – something to do with the atmosphere."

"Hover-fairies?" Jake shook his head slowly, in wonder. "Let me get this straight. You found these things, creatures, living in his house – and you've both kept it a secret ever since?" Jake looked around him, half expecting a wing to be poking out from under the sofa.

"No, they don't live here. But they do come here now and again."

"To watch TV?"

"Among other things."

There were other things? Other than the 'fact' of TV-watching hover-fairies?

Alva checked Strang, who was now snoring away. She turned to look at Jake.

"Can I trust you?" she said. "If I show you something?"

"A fairy?"

Jake was torn between thinking this whole thing was some kind of psychotic episode – whose psychosis, he wasn't yet sure – and the tantalising possibility that it was all true. In which case, he was about to see a fairy. Which, in turn, was obviously bonkers.

"Not exactly," said Alva. "They're not here at the moment. But you have to promise me something, if I show you. I mean it, it's important. Life-and-death important. You can never tell anyone."

"I promise."

Alva looked him squarely in the eyes, appraising his reply, and nodded. "Right, come with me," she said. "Don't worry about Ruan, he's out for the count now. I'll wake him later when I make his lunch."

Jake followed Alva out of the house, through a gate and into the woods.

Looking back, he got a view of the Strang place for the first time – a sprawling mansion, more than a mere house, with a main façade and a side wing. Not what he expected at all – he realised that he'd only seen a limited part of the property. And Strang owned all this, yet lived like he did? He could understand now why a hotel chain might want to buy it. Potential, it most definitely had.

When he turned, Alva was already ahead of him and calling for him to hurry up.

A narrow road descended through the trees, with steep, moss-covered rocks to either side. This must be the glen, which ran down to the beach at the head of the small loch. He caught up with Alva and they walked on for a few minutes.

"How did he get me all the way up to the house?" said Jake. "I don't remember walking any of this. I don't think I *could* have walked."

"I'd say he had help."

"What, from a couple of foot-high, so-called fairies?"

"Who said there were just a couple?" said Alva, which closed down that conversation.

The road ran out at the bay, where a curving, white-sand beach stretched out to either side, overlooked by cliffs. From here, he could look out along the sheltered inlet to the wider waters of the sound beyond and − barely visible on the horizon − the distant mainland. It was as secluded a spot as you could imagine, even if was only a couple of miles from Port Levin.

Alva led him onto the pier that he'd glimpsed from on high. It stretched out a good way over clear, blue water − Jake could see the bottom − which deepened and turned darker as they reached the boathouse at the end.

She took a key from her pocket and undid a padlock. Inside, under wooden rafters, the pier continued for twenty feet or more, open to the water beyond. A small rowing boat was tied up on one side. On the other, behind a short, wooden screen, was a rectangular metal casing unit with a hatch, that rose from the water and was set flush against the side of the pier.

Jake looked down into the water and could make out the first few feet of the metal structure as it disappeared into the darker depths.

He looked at Alva. "So?"

She took a deep breath. "You promised, remember?"

"I did. I mean, I do."

"It's an elevator," she said. "Down to their ship."

Chapter 15

Jake had been ready to abandon his non-job on Elsay and go home. In retrospect, that would have been the sensible move. Then he wouldn't have fallen off a cliff, banged his head, been locked in a trigger-happy drunk's house, rescued by a short-tempered Emma Stone lookalike, and told several impossible things that made no sense whatsoever.

The flip side, as he had to keep reminding himself over the next couple of days, were the following apparent facts:

There were fairies.

Who lived in a ship.

Under the water in a secret bay.

Which, when you put it like that, sounded like the plot from an Enid Blyton novel. Although he was still waiting to be offered lemonade and scones by a russet-cheeked farmer's wife, as opposed to being threatened with dismemberment with a shovel by a pissed recluse.

After the big reveal, Alva had not exactly clammed up, but she hadn't been any more forthcoming either.

Jake had said, "What do you mean, elevator?" and, "What do you mean, ship?" as any normal person would. Alva had deflected the conversation, as if she already feared she'd said or shown him too much.

They had walked back to the house in silence, whereupon Alva started bustling around, cooking and cleaning for Strang, and tried to persuade Jake to go back to Castle View and rest.

He was all for returning to the beach and looking for his phone, which still hadn't turned up in the house. It must be on the rocks somewhere. But Alva was adamant, and said she'd ask Strang to have a look, and keep an eye out for it herself.

Jake liked to think she was being solicitous about his health, but he could tell that she wanted him out of the way.

"You can't announce that there are fairies running around, and show me that – whatever it is – in the boathouse, and then just expect me to carry on with my day."

"I can," she had said. "I think I can trust you, though I don't really have a choice now. But this doesn't only affect me. I need to talk to Ruan, make sure he understands, and then I have to consult – someone else. It's not my decision alone."

"The General?"

Alva had looked startled. "Where did you hear that?"

"Something Ruan said on the beach. It didn't make much sense at the time. It still doesn't, to be honest."

Alva had shaken her head and closed her eyes briefly, like that was another problem she now had to deal with.

"Right," she had said. "Wednesday, come with me to the ferry to pick some things up. You can come back here afterwards and I'll show you then."

"Show me what?"

"It's easier if you see it yourself. But you need to give me a couple of days. And there's something I need you to do for me first."

Which is why, much against his better judgement, Jake was at the hotel on Wednesday, asking to borrow something again.

"The little wheely thing that moves boxes?" said Jimmy. The disdain dripped off him.

"Alva said you'd know what I meant? We need to borrow it."

"We?"

"Alva, then. She's picking up some things from the ferry, says it's easier with the wheely thingy."

"You want to borrow my sack barrow?"

"If that's what the little wheely thing's called."

"Jesus," said Jimmy, producing what looked like a ladder on wheels, with a flat metal plate set at ninety degrees. "Wheely thingy. Don't they teach you anything in England?"

By now, Jake knew that this was what passed for friendly banter.

"You can borrow it," said Jimmy, "but – "

"I know, if I prang it…"

"There would be ructions, English. Ructions." Ructions with at least four Rs.

At the quayside in the afternoon, Jake and Alva loaded more boxes into Duncan's van, with Jake delighted that for once he knew something that Alva didn't, namely the term sack barrow – not that she appeared impressed. Some of the boxes, they dropped at the hotel; the rest were apparently for Strang. "Supplies," said Alva, mysteriously, and didn't elaborate further.

Alva used her key to open the gate on the road, and they drove up to Strang's house, past the various 'Keep Out' notices that Jake now understood served a dual purpose.

"He put them up a couple of years ago," said Alva, "shortly after I came back. He's serious about them, thinks they keep people away from his house and land. Which they do, of course, because of the gate – and the fact that the road doesn't go anywhere else. At first, I was all for taking the signs down, seeing as they were attracting attention, but then I realised that they just fed into the narrative – that he's got a screw loose. Better people are laughing at him than thinking there really is something to hide."

They wheeled the boxes into the house through a side door and Alva disappeared with them into the kitchen for a while, leaving Jake with a clearly awkward Strang.

He had cleaned himself up a bit – trimmed his beard, by the look of things – and looked less mad, bad and dangerous to know than he had done a few days ago. The shotgun, Jake was relieved to see, was hanging on a sling from a hook by the door, and not being pointed in his face for once.

"Sorry," he mumbled to Jake. "About locking you in and everything. I couldn't be too careful, you know? But Alva, she says you're all right."

All right? That was encouraging, too. Until now, he'd mostly been in death-stare territory, as far as Alva was concerned.

The three of them walked down to the loch and the pier, and Alva unlocked the boathouse. Jake took the opportunity to have another look at the metal unit that descended into the water – not quite square, and eighteen inches wide on each side. Like a small laundry chute. If it was an elevator, as Alva had said, it wasn't big enough for a human to use. And how did it get here?

"They built it," said Alva. "At least, that's what they say. Ruan says he's never had any work done in here, and it is his boathouse, so he'd know." The old man nodded confirmation. "And it was already here when I first came."

"What's it for?"

"Told you, an elevator. So they can come up and down. Goes to an airlock, and then to the ship."

Jake inspected it again. The metal had a dull sheen but was otherwise featureless. No elevator buttons or display. Through an open hatch at the top, he could peer in and down – for maybe three or four feet. Couldn't even see where the water started.

"An elevator? Fairies need an elevator?"

"Well, they don't need it, exactly. It's just easier for them. More convenient."

"And when you say ship – ?"

"They call it a vessel. I'm assuming ship."

"You've not seen it?"

Alva, revisiting her more familiar death-stare persona, scoffed and pointed at the narrow metal unit. "You're welcome to try and get in."

"But – how do you know there's actually anything down there?"

"Because they told us. And where else do you think they come from?"

"How would I know?" Jake felt this conversation was beginning to go around in circles. "The woods. The glen. Flowerpots. Trees. Riding in on unicorns. They're fairies, aren't they?"

"I wouldn't get too hung up on the idea of actual fairies," said Alva.

"But you said!"

"I said that's what Ruan calls them, don't you?"

"It's the wee wings, Alva. And the way they move." Strang spread his fingers wide and waggled them. "You'll see!" he said.

"If they're not fairies, what are they? What do they need an underwater ship for?"

Questions you never thought you'd be asking, numbers seven and eight.

"That's what we're here to show you. All right, Ruan?"

The old man nodded and touched the facing side of the metal unit, just under the hatch. A tablet-sized screen lit up, with a row of illuminated symbols showing down the lefthand side. He tapped a green circle and the screen turned a fuzzy grey – like snow on a disconnected monitor.

Nothing else happened for what seemed like an age, and Jake couldn't say he was surprised. The whole thing, clearly, was mad.

He'd convinced himself he'd seen something on the beach a few days ago, but all he had to go on was the say-so of these two, neither of whom – for different reasons – seemed the most reliable of witnesses. There was no other evidence of any kind.

Maybe it was all a huge prank at the Englishman's expense – in which case, yes, brilliant, well done, he'd been fooled. Good one.

This metal chute – could be part of a fish storage tank? An inspection chamber of some kind? A fuel pump? How would he know? He hadn't even known what a sack barrow was until today.

Alva leaned forward and touched the green circle again. "Takes a while sometimes," she said.

Sure.

They stood for another minute, Jake wondering how he was going to extricate himself from this and still remain on reasonable terms. He hadn't forgotten Strang's shotgun, and the longer this went on, the more he wondered about Alva's state of mind. Never mind Strang's loose screw. She'd left university for a reason, and Fraser's assessment – that his daughter had had a breakdown – was looking more viable by the day.

The screen suddenly blinked and an alarm sounded – a beeping noise, which subsided after half a dozen tones. Then the fuzzy screen resolved itself into a view of a white-walled room – like they were looking at a CCTV image.

And front and centre of the room, looking directly at the screen, was a whiskered head and face atop a high collar, with shoulder epaulettes showing, and the unmistakable tips of wings rising behind.

"Ah, capital!" said the figure. "Lady Alva, Lord Strang. Delighted, as always."

Chapter 16

Jake simply stared at the screen, while Alva said, "Good to see you, General."

"This the blighter? Unkempt fellow from the beach?"

Jake took a second to realise that he was being talked about. To be honest, he was still getting his head around the 'Lady Alva, Lord Strang' business. And – backing up further –also coming to terms with the fact that there was some sort of winged creature addressing them. On a TV screen. From somewhere under the water. Was there anything he'd missed?

"He's a new ally, General," said Alva. "Ruan and I thought you should meet him. And we have your supplies."

"New ally, eh? I think I'll be the judge of that. Chap looks like an idle layabout, if you ask me." The General peered closely into the screen, and Jake flinched and took an automatic step backwards. "Sergeant! Prepare to beam us up!"

The screen turned a fuzzy grey again and then winked out.

Jake looked at Alva, who grinned. It was the first time he'd seen her look happy, so that was also disconcerting.

"Beam us up?" was all he could think to say in the moment.

"Ruan showed them *Star Trek*. They think Spock's ears are hilarious, though they can talk. Anyway, they're not actually going to beam up."

"What? They're coming up in that?" Jake gestured at the metal chute.

"On their way. The General wants to inspect you."

The unit began to emit a low hum, and a sequence of lights flashed across the screen. Alva and Strang stood back and beckoned for Jake to do the same.

The hum turned into a rumble, and the lights stopped flashing and formed a solid, horizontal line, which shortened segment by segment – over the space of perhaps a minute – until there was only one bar showing.

And then that disappeared, too, as the first creature popped out of the hatch. Followed by another and another and another – five in all – who appeared to hang briefly in the air in a flutter of wings before dropping into formation on the pier inside the boathouse.

Two stood on each side, facing Jake. The fifth strutted down the middle towards him. Off to one side,

Strang had visibly stiffened and was offering a three-fingered salute. Alva clasped her hands in front of her and had bowed her head. She elbowed Jake, who understood he was to do the same – eyes darting from side to side as he stared in disbelief at the scene.

The creatures came up to a point just below Jake's knee. He took an instinctive step backwards and tilted his head slightly for a better view. Not that that helped his understanding much.

'Creatures' was still his best reference point, but they were all wearing matching, tailored, dark-blue uniforms with coloured insignia, like pocket-sized fantasy warriors. The fifth one, in the middle, also had the high collar and fancy epaulettes that Jake had seen on the screen. The General, then.

Rugged, greyish skin, bushy facial hair, piercing eyes, flyaway eyebrows – and furled, bat-like wings that protruded from slits in the back of their tunics. The webbed tips still trembled slightly, which somehow was the most unnerving sight of all.

The uniforms ended in cuffs at ankle height, below which the creatures stood on bare, splayed feet that were more like eagle talons – yellowing ribs and ridges that ended in wicked-looking, curving, sharpened digits. The four creatures accompanying the General held foot-long batons that, with a click, extended to something like a lance, twice their height, as they formed an honour guard.

Fairies? If they were in a children's picture book, ongoing counselling would probably be required.

Perhaps a visit from social services to see which idiot parent had borrowed the book from the library in the first place.

Then again, it had only been Strang's word that they were fairies, and Strang was often drunk. And, presumably, had never seen the film *Gremlins*.

"Yes," said Alva, "I know."

Jake hadn't said anything and when he looked at her, he realised she wasn't speaking to him. She was looking directly down at the General instead.

"I couldn't persuade him of that," she said. "It seemed better this way. I think we can trust him."

There was a short silence and then Alva laughed. "I don't think we should do that," she said. "Too messy. Took me ages to clean up last time."

Jake felt something poke his thigh. The nearest creature prodded him again with his lance and gestured upwards, and Jake turned to find another of them hovering by his shoulder. Wings spread, barely fluttering. The hairy, gremlin face a foot or so from his own. A cupped, extended, claw-like hand presenting what looked like a tiny, brown vitamin tablet.

"Put that in your ear."

"Excuse me?"

"In your ear," said Alva.

"I'm not putting anything in my ear," said Jake. "What are you talking about? And what the −?"

He gestured at the sheer impossibility of what was going on around him. The flying creature. The gremlin guard of honour at his feet. The strutting General, whose own wings were now starting to unfurl, and whose wild, Eugene Levy eyebrows were doing some double-time manoeuvres.

"You will if you want to know what's going on. Don't be such a baby. Here."

She took the tiny tablet from the hovering creature's hand, nodded in acknowledgment, and poked it in Jake's ear before he had time to realise what she was doing.

"Hey!" He scrabbled with his finger but felt a slight slither in his ear, which stopped almost immediately. And then heard a voice.

"… simpleton?"

The General had joined his comrade in flight and was hanging midway between Jake and Alva. She laughed and shook her head.

"If you say so, Lady Alva, but the chap seems half-witted. Bit slow on the uptake. Not sure he'll be any use to us at all. You, sir. Yes, you."

The General had turned towards Jake, still hanging in the air. There was barely a movement from the wings, but they held the creature in place. And as Jake looked into the strange face, with its mass of whiskers and folds of skin, he realised that he was hearing it speak.

The voice wasn't in his head or being heard as if through an earpiece. The words were being spoken – he could see moving lips – and he could hear them, in the same way that he could hear Alva and Strang.

"There you go," said Alva. "Some kind of organic

transmitter and translation device, don't ask me how it works. You'll be able to communicate with all of them now. Oh, and talk normally, you don't need to shout, they don't like that."

"You're with us, are you? Excellent." The General fixed Jake with a glare, or possibly with his normal resting gremlin face, who knew? "I, sir, am General Zadar of the Second Fleet, formerly of Trogir in the Kotor System. And you are?"

"What?" said Jake, looking from the General to Alva and back again.

"What, sir!" said a chiding voice, seemingly from one of the creatures still on the ground.

"Apologies, General," said Strang, chipping in from the side-lines. "He's – "

"A simpleton, yes, quite. I see it now. The open mouth, the hairless cheek. Not one of your countrymen I take it, Lord Strang?"

"Him? The lad's a *sassenach*, General."

"Is he now? I don't like the sound of that. Are they all like this, the – Sassnacks? The weak chin, the pallid skin? And where are his whiskers, damn him? Has the man no pride? Servile class, I assume?" The General peered in more closely and tut-tutted.

"Who – *what* – are you?" Jake blurted out. Fairly coherent, under the circumstances. Talking to a hovering gremlin-fairy. Like that was a normal thing to be doing.

"Who are you, sir!" bellowed another voice from

below, accompanied by a sharp poke in Jake's ribs from a lance.

"Ow!"

"Doesn't like it up him, sir," said a third voice. "We could neutralise him now, just waiting for your order, sir!"

Jake looked down at the three creatures still on the ground, who had advanced in formation, brandishing their lances. The fourth – the one with the listening pill – had taken up a mid-air position by Jake's left ear and was reaching for the baton holstered on his back. Jake took a precautionary step backwards.

"What do you say, Lady Alva? Never trust a chap without whiskers, that's common sense. And this one seems particularly shifty to me? A Sassnack to boot, you say? They sound simply dreadful. We'd be better off neutralising the chap now, before he escapes."

Alva watched in amusement, before rescuing Jake, who had backed up as far as the boatshed door and could retreat no further.

"We won't be neutralising anyone today, General. I can vouch for him. Allow me to do the introductions. General Zadar, this is Jake. Jake, General Zadar." She looked meaningfully at Jake. "Now, salute him," she said quietly. "And don't say, 'What' anymore. And close your mouth. Trust me, this will all go much more smoothly if you show him some respect. He's a sweetie really, and sensitive when you get to know him, but he's a bit of a stickler for first impressions."

Chapter 17

"I don't even know where to start," said Jake.

He and Alva were walking across the beach, up towards the road into the glen, with the house beyond. Ahead of them were Strang and the five, small, winged creatures who wheeled and swooped around Strang's head.

They seemed to be playing, or at least enjoying the open air – diving and rising in formation, and then dropping to the ground to waddle alongside Strang, before lifting off again for another circuit around the old man.

"How about with, yes Alva, you were right, they do exist?"

Jake let that go, but she was right – the evidence was literally flying around in front of him.

"Where did they come from?"

"Ah, well, now you're asking."

"You mean you don't know?"

"Not exactly." Alva pointed up into the sky. "They're not from around here, I can tell you that."

Jake knew what she was saying. It didn't even seem a stretch, given what he'd seen so far. Bizarrely, it was probably easier to believe than the alternative – that fairies or gremlins, or whatever they were, actually existed.

But still, to say the word – out loud, in all seriousness – was yet another leap. Another acceptance of the incredible.

"Aliens?"

There, he'd said it.

"From Trogir in the Kotor System, apparently. You heard him."

"Which is where?"

"No idea. The General has tried to explain it, but he gets a bit bogged down in the technical details. Miles away, anyway. Billions of miles."

"But they're tiny!"

That seemed like a crucial point, though Jake wasn't sure why. He'd never stopped to think about aliens before – or, specifically, how big they ought to be.

"So is Yoda. Or what about ET?"

"Well, for a start, they're film characters, not real aliens. And then there's the fact that – " At which point Jake realised he had run out of arguments.

"What's your point? Look at them, they're real enough. And they came from somewhere, in a vessel, across the galaxy. What does their size matter?"

"They arrived in a spaceship?"

"That's what I understand them to mean. Vessel. Ship. Whatever."

"A spaceship that's now under water? In Scotland?" As he said it, Jake made the connection with something he'd heard elsewhere. "Wait, the tsunami? The thing your dad told me about? That was them?"

"I've always assumed so. Spaceship splashdown. The dates fit. Lucky it was at night – and a long way out at sea. There was never any evidence for anyone to find. Not that anyone bothered much, because there wasn't a whole lot of damage. It was a local-interest story, which fizzled out after a week or two."

"And then they just – what? Cruised in underwater and looked for a resting place? Fetched up near Elsay? Thought they'd stick around a while? Why?"

"That's a whole other story. I think I'll let the General tell you."

"He doesn't seem to like me that much."

"He needs to get used to you. You're only the third human he's met."

"After Lady Alva and Lord Strang? What's all that about?"

"That was Ruan's doing. He told them this was his land, and they seem to think he owns the whole planet. And when I turned up, they assumed I was part of his noble family. To be honest, it's easier to go along with it. They have some very funny ideas about how Earth works – partly because this is all they've seen of it. This bit of the island. That, and because of what they watch on TV."

"Dare I ask?"

"You'll see."

They reached the house, where Strang and the creatures were nowhere to be seen.

"They'll be inside," said Alva. "They come up every few days. They were due a visit anyway."

Jake remembered what Alva had said to the General in the boathouse. "For supplies?"

"Among other things," she said, pushing open the front door.

The large lounge room was as Jake had remembered, full of heavy, dark furniture. Light came in through a couple of deep bay windows, flanked by thick, plaid curtains that fell to the floor. Around the walls were framed paintings – island scenes and wildlife, mostly – and a set of gilt-edged, commemorative plates.

Photographs were arranged on an inlaid bureau – a young wedding couple on the steps outside a church, and another of a woman with kind eyes and a twinkly smile. The same woman as in the wedding picture, though perhaps forty years older. Strang's late wife, Eileen, presumably.

There was a coffee table with dog-eared magazines, the sofa that Jake had sat on and eaten a bacon sandwich, and twin armchairs orientated towards the TV. A pile of old videos was scattered across the floor in front of a vintage VHS player in a cabinet – movie classics and TV adaptations alike. *Pride and Prejudice, Zulu, Brideshead Revisited, Lawrence of Arabia, Jane Eyre, The*

Charge of the Light Brigade, Howards End, Far from the Madding Crowd, Great Expectations.

It was much as you'd expect of the house of an elderly widower who didn't want to change anything after his wife had died. Although presumably Eileen would have had something to say about the five aliens on the back of the sofa watching *Gulliver's Travels.*

"Neutralise the giant!" shouted one of them, as Lilliputians marched across Jack Black's chest, while he lay staked out on the sand.

"It's their new favourite," said Alva. "You can see why they freaked out when they saw you lying on the beach that day. The General wanted to deal with you there and then, except Ruan persuaded him that you might not remember anything after your bang on the head."

"Deal with me? Neutralise? With those itty-bitty sticks? They're only a foot high themselves. What are they going to do? Poke me severely?"

"You have no idea. I really wouldn't try and upset them. They got spooked by a seal on the beach last year and blasted it. There was blubber *everywhere.* You can still see the stains on the rocks."

Jake didn't know whether to believe her or not. Apart from the physical fact of there being five aliens in the house watching TV, he wasn't sure what he believed of the story.

Sure, some of it was starting to make sense. The archaic language, for example, that he'd heard from the General.

"They learned English from those?" He pointed at the videos.

"The way I heard it was, they followed Ruan up from the beach, the first time he met them. He was pissed, as usual, and thought he was seeing things. Came back, put on *Pride and Prejudice*, which was Eileen's favourite, and fell asleep with the bottle on his lap. When he came to, they were still there – only now they could talk to him."

"Via the little ear pill thing?"

"Exactly. And now you're up to speed," said Alva, heading out of the room. "I'm going to help Ruan. Watch TV with them, and don't annoy the General. Remember the seal."

Jake did not feel up to speed. Not even close. He stood nervously behind the aliens – the aliens! – and watched a few minutes of *Gulliver's Travels*, while the General occasionally swivelled his head around and fixed him with a disapproving glare. As if assessing him for neutralisation purposes.

A door opened, and Alva and Strang came back in, from somewhere down along a corridor. Strang was carrying a tray. "Dinner!" he called.

"Ah, capital!"

The General jumped from the back of the sofa, gliding with an imperceptible flutter of wings to the polished oval table on the other side of the room. The others followed, and they each perched on the edge as Strang set the tray on a raised wooden block in the centre of the table.

"Our vanquished foe, we salute you," said the General, who led the way, his claw-like hands darting to the tray and then to his mouth. Jake got a glimpse of razor-sharp teeth as each of the aliens fed themselves, occasionally plucking stray morsels from their beards.

"Are those — ? "

"Yes."

Alva really was infuriating. Jake widened his eyes and gestured — more information, if you wouldn't mind. She took him to one side, while they continued eating.

"They're self-sufficient on the ship. I don't know how exactly — lab-grown protein, some sort of produce farm. They're vague about it, but they obviously have their own food supplies. But when they first arrived here, they got a bit overexcited at the prospect of 'wild food' and wiped out Ruan's chickens. Thought they had defeated a fearsome predator and got a taste for the meat. And obviously, we couldn't keep buying live chickens — someone would have noticed."

"So, that's what the boxes from the ferry are?"

"Yup. Ruan had some in the freezer, and they seemed to like them. Wondered where the feathers were at first, but I told them they were from a different species. I order a few boxes now and again from the mainland. I suppose the ferry thinks they're for the hotel. And I tell these guys that I have a special contact with a big-game supplier."

The General hopped from the table, back to the

sofa. "Splendid, Lady Alva, as always. You're too kind. I'll send the rest of the crew up shortly."

Jake looked quizzically at Alva. Another case of not being up to anything approaching speed.

Until now, he hadn't thought about the logistics of flying an alien spaceship across the galaxy. How many people – things, creatures, aliens – might that require? What sort of numbers?

"Rest of the crew?"

"At least fifty of them," said Alva. "Why do you think I need so many boxes of chicken nuggets?"

Chapter 18

At a conservative estimate, Jake had a thousand questions. But they were going to get answered in Alva's own sweet time, while Strang hadn't been any more forthcoming. Except to say, "You see, you see!" a few times.

The General and his escort team had left, and Alva had steered Jake out of the house. "Ruan's going to deal with the rest of them. It takes all day because they can't leave the ship unattended," she had said.

And so Jake had been dropped back at Castle View that afternoon, while Alva went to work her shift at the hotel.

She had looked him in the eye before he got out of the van. Fixed him with a determined gaze.

"I know," he said.

"You can't say anything. Ever. I mean it."

"No one would believe me anyway."

"I'm serious. They've been kept a secret for nearly four years now. I'm trusting you."

"I know, it's OK. I promise."

Jake wasn't going to tell anyone. Admittedly, this was possibly the single greatest story in human history. But he wanted to know more, and he'd made a promise to a cute girl.

Hm. Well, she was cute, there was no denying it. And she had smiled at him again as she drove away. That was the second time today. Not that he was counting.

"There you are," said Duncan, as the van scrunched down the drive and disappeared. "Was that Alva? Never mind, I'll walk I suppose. Where have you been, anyway? I've been looking for you."

"Just out. Helping Alva," said Jake, keeping it vague, not that Duncan noticed.

"Good man. Right, I've left some paint in the lounge. Brushes, ladder, all that. Give it a couple of coats, will you? And give Alva another hand on Saturday in the shop? Trade's picking up, I can feel it."

Jake stood there, trying to work out what day it was, more than anything else, given the magnitude of what he'd seen and heard over the last few hours. But Duncan apparently mistook his silence for a negotiating tactic, because he reached into his pocket for his wallet, took out two – no, three – twenties, and said, "All right, will this cover you until the weekend?" He didn't wait for a reply, and sauntered off down the driveway.

Jake spent the next two days painting the reception rooms in the main house at Castle View, and took his meals as usual up at the hotel. If he saw Alva there, she avoided his eye or glared a warning, and Jake got it – no discussion of our undersea alien friends in a public place.

He had to wait until the Saturday, when they were together again at the shop, before he could even raise the subject, and even then it was difficult because Duncan kept coming and going.

"I've been on the Instagram, darling," he said to Alva. "Or TikTox, one of them, anyway. Posting, I've been. Tagging and reeling."

"Oh God, tell me you haven't?"

"Wait till the influencers cotton on to these beauties, they'll be flocking here," and he unboxed fifty XL T-shirts with a picture of the Pope brandishing a gladiator's trident in the Colosseum and a speech bubble that said, 'You talkin' to me?'

Duncan pinned one to a wall to display it, and talked in upbeat terms about the summer season ahead. He'd been buoyed by the previous week's sales – pitiful though they seemed to Jake – and reckoned visitor numbers might finally be on the increase again.

"About time," he said. "Been a hard few years. Maybe I'll get Jimmy to open up a couple of the letting rooms at the hotel again – for the cyclists and hikers, you know? Advertise down at the ferry?"

"Is he always this optimistic?" said Jake, when Duncan had finally left them alone for the day.

"The word is delusional," said Alva. Then her face

softened. "He's a dreamer. A hopeless one really, but that's just how he is. The thing about Dad – "

She paused, and Jake noticed the word she had used. He'd only ever heard her call him Duncan before.

"Is that he's always looking for an opportunity. A wheeze. A break. Something he can make money from. If I'm here, at least I can try and head off the more disastrous ideas." She nodded at the T-shirts. "Try, anyway."

Jake understood what she was saying. "The wee fellas?"

Alva wrinkled her nose. "Can you imagine what Duncan would do if he knew about them? The schemes he'd hatch? What the village might do? The biggest story in the world? They would think they'd won the lottery."

"You're protecting them? That's why you've stayed?"

"It was an accident, that I found them, met them. I came back from college two years ago for the summer and there they were – miraculously undiscovered because Ruan's an old soak who no one listens to."

"Your dad thinks you haven't gone back because of your anxiety. Your health." As he said it, Jake realised the truth.

"How could I leave, after knowing what I know? You've met Ruan. He can't be trusted with them on his own. And what would happen to the General – to all of them – if they were found? They'd be captured, whisked away, locked up, exhibited, who knows? Or the entire island would be sequestered and we'd all be moved out. You just know what would happen if the world discovered there were aliens here, and none of it would be good. It would be out of our hands."

"So you've stayed and kept them a secret? Tried to put people off?"

Including himself. She hadn't been particularly welcoming at any point, and maybe that was simply the way she was? Not a people person. But it would certainly explain why she'd been so frosty with him from the start. Concerned that he was coming to the island in the first place, and staying on, even though there wasn't a real job for him? Worried about what he might find out?

And then Jake realised there was even more to this. "That's why Ruan turned down the offer for his land? That's why you supported him? Maybe even persuaded him to turn it down?"

Alva sighed, deeply. "I felt awful. Still do. Objectively, it would have been great for the island. There would have been jobs. Duncan might have got his business back. But Ruan never wants to leave that house. You've seen it, it's a shrine to Eileen. And we can't risk anything that brings more visitors here. It's the only way to keep them safe, whatever the islanders think of me – and however much people like Duncan and Jimmy struggle to make a living."

Hearing it spelled out like that – that would have been a heavy burden to bear. No wonder she was like she was. Anxiety wasn't the half of it. She must have been living in constant fear, with no end in sight.

"You can't stay here for ever, though?"

"Why not? It is my home."

"What about the next time someone happens to see them? Or the next business proposal? You really think you can carry on hiding them?"

"I don't know. I'm going to try. They're special. And that makes this a special place now."

"Maybe. But you don't even know what you're protecting."

"What do you mean? You've seen them. I've told you about them."

"I've seen a few creatures – aliens, maybe – that I can't explain. How many of them are there? How big is this ship? You've never even seen it. How far down is it, if there's anything there at all? Where did it come from? Who are they? Why are they here? What do they want?"

"That's a lot of questions."

"Well, it's a lot you're asking me to keep secret. I only came here for a summer job. I didn't expect to end up in Roswell-on-Sea."

"They're Trogirans."

"What?"

"Trogirans. That's what they call themselves. From the planet Trogir. I've seen maybe fifty in total, but I think there are more in some kind of deep-sleep stasis. The ship was part of a fleet and got separated from the others. The water out in the sound reaches a thousand feet deep in parts, which is why you can't see the vessel. And now you know as much as I do."

It still didn't seem like a lot that you could be certain about. Was it enough to change your whole life for?

"And you're the Lady Alva?"

She finally smiled at that. Third time today. Though there was a tinge of sadness in it, too.

"That's the best bit," she said. "Duncan says my mum used to call me her little princess. I can't remember it, but I reckon she'd love that I've become a lady."

Chapter 19

Jake went up with Alva to Strang's house again on the Monday, even though she told him the Trogirans wouldn't be there.

"It's risky for them to come up very often," she said. "You'll have to wait to see them again. In any case, they have a whole spaceship to live on. It's enormous. Like a city in the sky. Or underwater now, as it happens."

"How is that even possible? How big can it be? I mean, given the size of them?"

Jake spent a fruitless afternoon trying to figure out the technical specifications of a spaceship piloted by short-arse aliens.

The internet was not helpful, especially the painfully slow variety that could be accessed on Ruan Strang's ancient computer, used only occasionally for the "wee electric letters." It was never a good sign when a PC was covered with a dust sheet and had a plant pot on top.

Anyway, say the Trogirans were roughly a sixth of his size – a foot high to his six foot? That meant that their spaceship might be a sixth the size of a regular human spaceship, whatever that was? All Jake had to go on was the International Space Station, which apparently was "larger than a six-bedroomed house" and had a crew of seven. Jake supposed that – for six Trogirans to a human – you could multiply seven by six, giving forty-two, which was close enough to Alva's guess of at least fifty crew on the Trogiran ship.

But the International Space Station was not a trans-galactic vessel. It looked like a glorified TV aerial and just pootled around the earth sixteen times a day. And it was pretty cramped in there.

No, you'd need something much bigger and more spaceshippy for a long voyage – probably more like the USS *Enterprise*. But Ruan's *Star Trek* videos were surprisingly unhelpful on the subject. There would be Trekkie websites devoted to the matter, for sure, but how far down a nerd-filled rabbit hole did he want to go? Not that far.

Whatever. If there was anything down there, however big, it was well hidden in hundreds of feet of dark water. He'd have to be patient, until the Trogirans decided to show themselves again.

Instead, Jake helped Alva clean Ruan's house, for something to do. He had a good look for his phone, and even went back down to the beach and searched among the rocks where he'd fallen, but to no avail. He'd have to get a new one, but apparently that meant taking a ferry over to the mainland, and catching at least two buses to a town large enough to have a phone shop.

"I could buy one online and get it delivered?" he'd said, and Alva had scoffed at the notion that he thought that was even possible. Although it was a bit rich that an alien spaceship could find its way to Elsay, but you couldn't get a courier service to deliver one small package.

On the following day, Tuesday, he hung out with Alva in the hotel kitchen while she prepped for the upcoming music night – funk n' soul with Jimmy the landlord's Average Shite Band. He even chopped a few vegetables and watched over a simmering stock.

While she was cooking, Alva was more relaxed. Less snippy. Seemed more content – or at least distracted from her worries. Meryl-Streep *Julie and Julia* Alva was a considerable improvement on heat-seeking-missile, *La Femme Nikita* Alva.

And on the Wednesday, Jake was back working in the gift shop, rearranging some of the displays. The papal-gladiator *Taxi Driver* T-shirts had not troubled the till at the weekend, and Jake and Alva exchanged knowing glances as Duncan delved around in the store-room for something more likely to change his fortunes.

"What?" he said, when he caught sight of them.

"Nothing!" They both laughed – a nice, complicit laugh.

Buoyed by his surprisingly enjoyable day with Alva, Jake went up to the hotel early that evening. Have a drink with Duncan before the music started, see if he might get paid for another job.

All thoughts of leaving were now temporarily abandoned. There were unforeseen compensations for this largely non-paying job in the middle of nowhere – none that he could share with Duncan or anyone else, but he could at least make it look like he was keen to work.

Duncan was already there, of course, at his usual booth. Jimmy was behind the bar and nodded a greeting.

"Sit, sit," said Duncan. "Just the man. Jimmy, a drink for the lad."

Jake sat opposite Duncan, and Jimmy brought over a pint of Little Widdle. "On the house," he said, unexpectedly.

"Really? Thanks."

"Sure," said Jimmy, and wedged himself in beside Jake. It was like being book-ended by a WWE wrestler.

"Enjoying it here, Jake?" said Duncan. "Thinking of sticking around?"

"Erm, I suppose so. If there's the work, you know?"

"We do what we can, Jake. We do what we can. And you don't have a girlfriend to get back to? Boyfriend, maybe?"

"No," said Jake, carefully. Not knowing at all where this was going.

"Good, good." Duncan seemed relieved. "You like the scenery, though, I take it? Plenty here to interest you, if you get my drift?"

The scenery? Plenty to interest him? Did Duncan know something? Jake took a sip of his drink to buy some time.

"I suppose," he said. What could he admit to liking that wouldn't sound lame? That wouldn't give the game away about the presence of aliens in the next bay? "It stays light until late in the evening, I'm not used to that. And there's the harbour and castle, and everything. Different to London, you know?"

Well, that was a terrible answer, but it would have to do.

"Only Jimmy here reckons you've been spending quite a lot of time with Alva? That right, Jimmy?"

"Aye." The big man leaned in, his massive thigh squashing against Jake's.

Oh, god. Was *this* what this was about?

"You know, helping her at the ferry, or up at Ruan Strang's old place. In the shop, here and there, joking and chatting. And there's not a lot of money in that for you, so Jimmy reckons you're maybe staying for other reasons now?"

Oh, dear god.

Jake took another deep drink of Little Widdle, avoiding any eye contact. He could feel the colour rising in his cheeks.

"Now, how long would you say you've known our Alva, Jimmy?"

Another hefty squish of the thigh, as the bulky landlord considered the question.

"Since she was a wee bairn, Duncan. Lovely little thing, she was."

"She is lovely, isn't she? Takes after her mum, god rest her soul. Very pretty. Kind to others. Heart of gold, mostly."

"Very pretty," said Jimmy.

"And you're a nice lad, Jake. A hard worker."

"English," said Jimmy.

"Well, there is that," said Duncan, "but even so, entirely normal that you'd take a shine to our Alva."

Please. Make. This. Stop.

"I haven't – I mean, I wouldn't – " Jake floundered. "I don't even think she likes me."

"Oh, she likes you, Jake. It's obvious. Hardly shouts at you at all, I've noticed. So's Jimmy."

Jake kept his silence, hoping this would all be over soon. Or that it was a bad dream. Because if it wasn't a bad dream, he'd be having nightmares about this conversation for the rest of his life.

"Aye," said Jimmy, taking over. "So, here's the thing. We love our Alva – mostly, when she's not yelling at us about something or other. Love her to bits. Our little princess. And we just want to see her happy."

"But, you know, she's had a tough time this last couple of years," said Duncan. "Left university, not feeling herself. You know how it is sometimes?"

"Understood," said Jake, heeding the warning. "Got it. Don't worry. Loud and clear."

And, dear god, let this be over now.

"So, it's fine if you want to get friendly with her,"

said Jimmy. "Take her out on a date, maybe. A nice walk, picnic, something like that."

What the actual –

"She has Thursday nights off," said Fraser. "Here at the hotel."

"That's right," said Jimmy. "Thursday is a good day for a date. But if you – "

Oh. My. God. Please don't say, 'Prang her.'

"Mess her about," said Duncan. "Upset her, anything like that, you'll have us to deal with."

He sat back and smiled, and Jimmy clapped Jake on the shoulder in a sort of Vulcan nerve pinch, before sliding back out of the booth.

"Good," said Duncan. "I think we're all on the same page here. Now, Jimmy, another drink, it's the lad's round. I'll have a double."

Chapter 20

That was a conversation Jake was never going to mention to Alva. Ever.

He also didn't know whether he'd been subjected to the old reverse psychology trick by the pair of them. Well played, if so, because the more Alva opened up to him – seemingly relieved that the secret was out – and the more she smiled rather than scowled at him, the more Jake recalled Jimmy's overbearing thigh, his mighty build and his Vulcan death grip.

Ruan Strang had mellowed towards him, too, content to have him up at the house when Alva was there without reaching for his shotgun. Or his shovel.

He wasn't drinking as much, either, and was positively chatty at times, though Jake couldn't always follow the thread.

"Have to keep the wee fellas hidden, safe," Ruan said. "Very important."

"Sure. Of course. I'm not going to tell anyone."

"In hiding, you know?" Ruan tapped his nose, conspiratorially. "Heads down, nice and quiet. Can't be found."

"I understand."

"Until, you know, one day... " Ruan made an upward motion with his hand.

"One day what?"

"Whoosh," said Ruan. "If their wee pals, you know... ?"

"What?" said Jake, but Ruan had already beetled off into another room.

Later, Ruan came into the kitchen, where Alva and Jake were flattening down chicken nugget boxes, prior to stacking them in an outbuilding. There were scores in there already. "Keep meaning to burn them," said Alva. "Can't exactly recycle them, without a load of questions."

"Exercises, Alva," said Ruan, interrupting them.

"What day is it?" she said. "Oh yes, you're right. Why not take Jake?"

"Exercises?"

"Got to be ready. You never know," said Ruan, tapping his nose again.

"You'll see," she said. "Go with him. And don't annoy the General."

You'll see, don't annoy the General, and other gnomic utterances. That was the extent of his life now.

He followed Ruan down to the boathouse. The old man scanned the beach and the surrounding cliffs before unlocking the door. Secluded, silent, save for the 'keow' of a swooping gull. The high, jagged rocks and tumbling gorse on either side kept the sands largely hidden from above, while any boats passing the entrance to the loch were a long way distant.

Not for the first time, Jake wondered about the so-called elevator. It could hardly go straight down from the boathouse, the water wasn't deep enough at that point. It had to go down and out – a long way out into the sound, where the deepest water was? More of a tunnel than an elevator? And if so, how did that work?

Inside the boathouse, Ruan touched the side of the chute, brought up the screen, and pressed a combination of symbols. The screen flickered, briefly showed a uniformed creature – not the General – who acknowledged Ruan's presence, and then the countdown line appeared.

Another minute went by, accompanied by a humming noise, and the creatures started appearing as before – popping out of the chute into the air, and fluttering imperceptibly to the ground.

This time, there were more of them. Many more. Jake counted twenty, and they didn't line up on the internal boardwalk, but headed for the open door, the pier and the beach beyond. All dressed in similar uniforms, though with different flashes and patches – for ranks? – and a wide range of tones and streaks in their bountiful facial hair.

The General popped out last. Ruan sprang to attention and saluted and Jake, to his surprise, found himself doing the same, though felt self-conscious about it.

"Lord Strang!" The General boomed a welcome. "I see you've kept the Sassnack on? Matter for you, of course. I suppose it's difficult to find good servants. Keep him on a tight leash, that's my advice."

"Servant? I'm not a servant."

"Well, you're not a gentleman, sir!" The General roared at the very idea. "Where's your whiskers, damn your eyes!"

Jake put his hand to his chin. This again. Maybe it would be worth not shaving for a week or two, if it would mollify the intergalactic squirt.

"Before we begin," said the General, "I'd like to return the Sassnack's personal device for your safe-keeping, Lord Strang." He presented a small, oblong, metallic box and laid it at Ruan's feet. "We found it on the beach. Primitive, of course, but even so I would be wary of allowing technology in such hands."

"Is that my phone in there?" Jake reached down for the box but got a rap on the knuckles with a baton for his troubles.

"Your Sassnack had highly suspicious surveillance images of our location on this device, Lord Strang. Not to mention some frankly scandalous images of other chaps – whiskerless, of course, goes without saying – standing in the water dressed in nothing but short pantaloons. And there seems to be an archive of what are described as musical offerings, but when we accessed it we couldn't discern a single tune. Just a lot of shouting and banging."

OK, so they'd found last year's holiday snaps and his Spotify playlists.

"Anyway," said the General, "I had my scientist chappies denude the device, for safety purposes, and place it in this surge-cage. You must do with it what you will."

Jake didn't like the sound of 'denude' or 'surge-cage.' He grabbed the box, which rattled as he picked it up. Inside, were several small pieces of metal, scattered screen shards, a pile of black dust, a few tiny screws, a mangled circuit board, and a bent, cracked SIM card.

"Come on, come on," said the General, buzzing a couple of feet off the floor. "Let's get the chaps started."

They left the boathouse, with Jake the last out, still looking forlornly at the bits of his phone. The General turned around and barked "Door!" at him. "He really will need some proper training, Strang."

"Not a servant," said Jake again, under his breath, but closed the door anyway.

"And don't mumble, man! A simple 'Yessir' will do."

So far, Jake wasn't seeing any sign of the General being a sweetie. And he owed him a phone.

On the beach, the other wee fellas had organised themselves into groups of four and were taking up positions on the sand, two versus two.

They advanced on each other using their shortened batons and skirmished in a flurry of whirls and clacks, leaving scuffed talon marks on the beach. They took it in turns being airborne, to offer another point of attack

– and defence – and occasionally one of the creatures tumbled out of the melee, shaking its head, caught by an undefended blow.

"What am I looking at here?" said Jake, at the extraordinary spectacle.

"Their little exercises," said Strang, beaming but unhelpful. "Aye, just look at them go. At it like the clappers, they are."

"Combat training," clarified the General. "We never know if or when the day will come. Our enemies could be close, and we must be ready."

"Enemies?" said Jake. "You mean the chickens?"

"The Earth beasts?" scoffed the General. "No, Sassnack, we vanquished those on arrival. Extremely poor adversaries. They were no match for our might."

Well, that's because they were domesticated chickens – but pointing that out probably came under the category of annoying the General, so Jake let it go. But he still wasn't clear who the enemy was.

"Who – what – then?"

"Who do you think, man? The Niksic. The reason we're here, flung out across the galaxy, far from the shores of Trogir. Do try and keep up. Are you sure, Lord Strang, that the Sassnack has the mental capacity for all this?"

The General puffed himself up to his full height – maybe fourteen inches – and strutted off down the beach. Jake could hear him issuing a command to stop, followed by further instructions, after which the creatures reassembled in different configurations and started fighting again. Now they seemed to be in two opposing phalanxes, and had extended the batons into lances, probing for gaps in each side's flank.

"The Niksic?" said Jake.

"Oh, the wee fellas don't like them at all," said Ruan. "Terrible, they sound. Cruel, too. Drove our wee fellas off their planet. And here they are, in their hidey vessel, under the water. Got to keep it a secret, see. Nice and quiet, so the other wee fellas can't find them."

"The Niksic are like them, you mean? You know?" Jake searched for a better word and gave up. "Short. Gremliny?"

"Hm? I suppose so." Ruan looked as if he'd never considered this before. "Anyway, they do their wee exercises, so they'll be ready for them. If the time comes. That's what the General says."

Jake looked at the hand-to-hand combat taking place in front of him and tried to picture how an inter-fairy-gremlin battle might unfold.

He supposed they could brain each other with their minuscule batons, or overpower a straggler at close quarters, but honestly, it was ridiculous. They were a foot tall, for Christ's sake! And presumably could fly away at the first hint of trouble – though Alva had said they struggled to gain much height in Earth's atmosphere.

None of it made a great deal of sense, although for the first time Jake had a hint of an explanation for their presence.

The Trogirans, it seemed, were on the run. An alien

race, hiding out under Scottish waters in a spaceship they were concealing from an arch enemy. Real science-fiction stuff, though Jake doubted anyone could make this up.

Seriously, look at them.

Buzzing around in their little uniforms, buffeting each other with sticks, commanded by a half-pint general who spoke like a Victorian squire. Flown across the galaxy in a ship no one had seen. Being concealed by a lapsed student, an old recluse, and now him. He really did have to take a lot of this on faith and, at this point, Jake was again uncertain what he believed.

One of the Trogiran lances had been jettisoned from the training session and lay on the sand near him. It was a couple of feet long and, when he picked it up, apparently made of some sort of lightweight metal. Jake held it out in front of him, Harry Potter-like. He'd seen them extended and retracted using a button on the side, and he clicked it twice, watching the lance turn into a foot-long baton and then a two-foot lance again.

That was neat. But the Niksic didn't have much to worry about as far as he could see. It didn't even have a pointy end.

"Put that wand down!" The General had noticed and was shouting. "You haven't had the training."

Wand! He had to be kidding. Give it a rest, beardy. They'd be better off learning how to use Ruan's shotgun, though it would probably take three of them to pull the trigger.

"Put it down now!" roared the General. "And don't, under any circumstances – "

The rest of the sentence was lost in an ear-splitting crack, followed by a short silence, and then a much longer, explosive retort that echoed across the bay.

"Don't force the slide-mechanism on the hilt," presumably, which was what Jake had done when his thumb had encountered a stubborn nub on the lance. The safety catch?

He'd been facing away from the group on the beach, which was something. The combat teams were largely unharmed.

Not so the giant boulder a hundred feet away, at the foot of the northern cliff. That was currently in a million tiny pieces, falling in shards across the sand and on top of an angry General and twenty of his startled crew.

"That's done it," said Ruan. "Not again."

Chapter 21

"What were you thinking?" said Alva.

Not the lovely, kind Alva with a heart of gold that Duncan had mentioned. The Alva with capital A attitude; the one whose glare could down aircraft at ten thousand feet.

"I didn't think they had actual weapons. I mean, look at them."

"I told you about the seal on the beach."

"I thought you were joking."

They were back at Ruan's house. Most of the Trogiran crew had bolted for the sanctuary of the boathouse and hopped into the elevator chute. Just in case, according to Ruan – they couldn't be too careful. But even if the noise had been heard in the village, or out on the water, it might have been assumed to be a rockfall. They weren't uncommon.

Two crew had stayed with the General, and they'd prodded Jake back up to the house. Now he'd seen what the lances could do, he didn't dally. But equally, he didn't see how any of this was his fault.

"He's very upset," said Alva, meaning General Zadar, who was in the lounge with Ruan. Jake didn't doubt it – he'd heard the phrase, "Neutralise the blighter" more than once on the way up. And he now understood what being neutralised entailed. Maybe the Niksic ought to be worried?

Still, how was he to have known? They were just wee fellas with wings and wands.

"That's the problem, isn't it?" said Alva. "You still don't really believe it?"

"I think I've moved beyond that," said Jake. "I mean, there's a foot-high astro-gremlin with whiskers in the lounge, watching *Little House on the Prairie*. He's hard to ignore."

"That's what I'm talking about. You don't take it seriously. Don't fully believe that they are what they say they are?"

Maybe that was the case? It was a stretch – the whole business. That they were aliens was slightly more believable than that they were fairies, but what kind of a benchmark was that?

"I know how it looks," said Alva. "How *they* look. But it's happening. They're here. You have to get over the size thing, or the wings, if that's what it is. Their technology is far ahead of ours. Their species has built star ships and crossed the galaxy. They've got engineers and scientists on board. The General was responsible for the security of an entire planet and blames himself every day for the fall of Trogir. He couldn't prevent the Niksic invasion. He's seen his escaping colony fleet scattered and he's reliant on strangers – aliens, us – to hide his ship from his enemies. They can't ever be found. We mustn't do anything to give them away. It would be the end of them."

There was colour in her cheeks and an urgency in her voice. But she wasn't angry – at least, not with him. She was passionate. For her, this was a cause. This was why she had given up on university and stayed on the island. She was protecting refugees. Alien refugees.

Jake had the good sense not to make a joke of any of it. This Alva, he liked. The Alva who combined attitude with a heart of gold.

"All right," he said, finally. "I'm sorry. I'll be more careful."

"Give me a minute," said Alva. "Let me see if I can smooth things over. I think we need to start again."

"It would help if he didn't treat me like an imbecile."

"A Sassnack, you mean?" She pronounced the word as the General did and grinned. "It's a synonym for idiot, didn't you know?"

"Very funny."

Jake stayed where he was, while Alva went next door to talk to the General. He could hear voices, though not what was being said, and was eventually called in.

The General was in his usual position, on the back of the sofa. Ruan was sitting in an armchair, with a crew member on either armrest, looking settled and cosy. Alva called Jake over as he came through the door.

"I've explained to General Zadar that it was an unfortunate accident. That you are fully committed to the cause. And, in fact, an equal member of our team, with useful skills of your own."

Jake hoped he wouldn't be asked to enumerate those, but he'd take the compliment.

"Yes, well," harrumphed the General. "It seems, Sassn—"

Alva gave him a plane-downing stare.

"Jay-kuh," said the General, unconvincingly, having a first stab at his name. "Lady Alva tells me that you can be fully trusted. Lord Strang, too. And perhaps I have been a little quick to judge." The General shook his head. "But that face, dammit! How you can expect anyone to take you seriously, without the whiskers…" He caught sight of Alva again. "Anyway, where was I? Oh yes, perhaps a short briefing might help? Put you in the picture, so to speak? Good idea, yes? Capital."

Jake sat and listened. The picture was extraordinary.

The Kotor System was a stable federation of planets in a distant spiral of the galaxy, thousands of light years from Earth. The Trogirans had lived and traded there for millennia, as had various other races, and with prosperity and security had come technological advance. Equally shared, benefitting all.

But the rise of the Niksic, a warrior caste from the

outer rim, had threatened the integrity of the system. They were imposing and aggressive – the General raised his claw-like hands above his head to indicate their relative height, two or three inches above his own. And they shaved their whiskers – shaved them! – before battle. "As if to mock us!" said an indignant General.

The Niksic had been stalled for a while, by treaty and appeasement. But with their own, marginal, planet's resources dwindling, they had advanced on the system proper and had taken anything in their path. Including Trogir, which had been abandoned by its allies in the face of overwhelming force.

"They took everything," said the General. "Trogir was theirs. Our defences were overrun, and I was tasked with leading an exodus fleet, in the hope that we could find sanctuary elsewhere. But our neighbours closed their borders, not wanting to antagonise the Niksic further, and we were forced to jump to deep space, and keep jumping to evade Niksic battle scouts. The colony vessels of the fleet were scattered. I failed."

The General's tone had changed. He sounded bereft.

"And your ship landed here, on Earth?" said Jake. "Why? How?"

"We are lost souls, Jake. Once separated from the others, yet still pursued by the enemy, we made a final jump and emerged in your system. It seems peaceful, largely uninhabited, technologically undeveloped. Your species has shown us kindness, and your water world presents a barrier to discovery by Niksic search probes, were they to find the system. And so we stay hidden, while our scientists scan the galaxy for signs of my fleet."

"And?"

"The void is silent, thus far. We may be the last of the Trogirans. We have no home to return to. We stay hidden or we die."

There was a sombre silence. The TV was off. Ruan was still sitting in his chair, and Alva had moved to the sofa. Jake looked her in the eye and shook his head slightly at the magnitude of it. Understanding fully for the first time. Believing fully for the first time.

"You can count on me, General," he said. Meaning that fully, too, for the first time.

"Excellent. Then we shall say no more about today's regrettable incident." The General stepped off the back of the sofa and hovered. "Chaps?" he said, and then hesitated, as he saw what was going on. "Ah, yes, of course," he said in a much lower voice to Jake. "We'll let Lord Strang finish."

Ruan was sitting in his armchair, holding a framed photograph on his lap. One of the ones from the mantelpiece – Jake could see a black-and-white picture of a young woman in a party dress. Standing on the floor beside him, at knee height, the two Trogiran crew members each had a clawed hand touching the frame and another holding Ruan's free hand.

Ruan had a half-smile that broadened, and Jake saw him gulp. Tears welled in his eyes, and he blinked once, twice.

"It's beautiful," said Alva, watching. "Every time."

"You see, Jake," said the General, almost whispering. "We understand loss. We understand what it means when your world is taken away from you."

"Ah, Eileen," sighed Ruan. "Where have you been, my love? Such a dancer, you were. And me with my two left feet. But you never minded."

"The pain is in the absence," said the General. "The not knowing. The not seeing. And hiding away, while necessary, cuts us off from our feelings."

Was he talking about Ruan Strang, or himself? Perhaps both.

"But feeling is living, Jake. Feeling is remembering. Feeling is seeing. And if we can help others feel, see and remember, why wouldn't we do that for our friends?"

Ruan was crying softly now. "Ah, my wee pals," he said. "My wee pals, thank you."

The General leaned across from his hovering position and lightly touched Jake's ear — the one where the little pill had been deposited, days previously. And then Jake saw it, too.

A young woman in the middle of the room in a party dress and dancing shoes. A young woman with tumbling brown hair and a sparkling ring on her finger.

"Eileen, my love," said the old man, wiping away a tear.

She flickered and pulsed, like a projected image, but was round and real, and full of life. Her red pumps on the worn rug; her white dress quivering in the airless room. Light in her eyes and colour in her cheeks.

"Shall we?" said Ruan and stood, offering a hand. "I'll try not to step on your foot." The woman smiled – from a deep well of affection, from a lifetime of togetherness – and took her husband's hand in hers.

And they danced.

Chapter 22

The revelations changed everything for Jake, but at the same time they brought a period of normalcy and routine to his time on Elsay.

There was a wonder about the presence of the little aliens. He saw that now. He understood why Strang and Alva had invested everything in hiding and protecting them.

Even so, he still couldn't fully get his head around the magnitude of what he'd been shown. One of the great questions for humankind – is anyone out there? – answered by the appearance of a tiny, technologically advanced species in a remote Scottish loch.

Out there – or rather, here – they certainly were, with a culture and a story of their own, and powers that he couldn't comprehend. Only three people on Earth knew that aliens incontrovertibly existed, and he just happened to be one of them. The responsibility was immense.

On the other side of the balance was the fact that he was a student who had come to Elsay for a summer job. He didn't belong here, and it wasn't the job he had been promised – on some days, it was barely a job at all – but there was enough in it to keep him busy. Which gave him enough cover to still be on the island.

Plus, both Duncan and Jimmy were convinced that he was only sticking around because of Alva, so that gave Jake even more of a purported reason to stay on Elsay. Although it did mean putting up with Jimmy giving him the eye-V-sign, pointy finger, 'I'm watching you' routine, every time he left the hotel bar.

Even Mrs Dunmore at the shop seemed to be in on it. After dispensing her usual cry of "Tally ho!" at him one day, when Jake came in to buy teabags and milk, she said, randomly, "Lovely girl, Alva, don't you think?"

"I suppose," he said carefully, wondering who she'd been talking to.

"Suppose, tish tosh, I've seen the way you look at her."

Warily, tinged with apprehension, like the way you'd eye an active volcano, mostly, though Jake still blushed.

He did look at her, of course he did. No one ever said she wasn't attractive. That whole Emma Stone vibe – you couldn't help but notice. Especially thrown together on an island where the next person in age was about fifty.

"I don't know what you mean," he said, thinking that was the safest response.

"Course you don't, dearie." She nodded sagely. "Honestly, young men, staring them in the face and they still don't know when someone's sweet on them."

Sweet? Alva? Really? On what planet?

"I don't think so," he said. But what did he know? He was no good at this sort of stuff.

"I wouldn't be too sure, English. I've known Alva Fraser since she was a baby, and while her mother chose an idiot, young Alva has got her head screwed on. Knows what she wants, that one."

This was all headline news, as far as Jake was concerned – not least that Duncan was confirmed as the island idiot – but he couldn't imagine for one minute that Mrs Dunmore had got it right.

He said what he'd said previously to Duncan and Jimmy. "I don't even think she likes me that much."

"Oh dear, you really haven't been paying attention, have you? I hope you're not going to disappoint me, young English?"

"Pardon?"

"Faint heart never won fair lady," said Mrs Dunmore, handing him his change. "And don't you worry about Duncan Fraser and Jimmy McPherson, the big lump. They're both as daft as each other. They give you any trouble, you come straight to me."

Who *had* she been talking to? Or, more to the point, where had she secreted the listening devices?

There was a lot about island life that Jake realised he didn't know. But whichever way you looked at it, he now had valid reasons to be on Elsay, coming and going in the company of Alva. And, as a consequence, no one thought it odd that Jake was now also spending more time up at Ruan's house. In fact, Duncan was relieved.

"He's never let anyone else up there," he said. "Not since Eileen died, anyway. I've never been sure about our Alva going there, to be honest. On her own, you know? Just as well you're around to give her a hand. Look after her."

Look after her? Had Duncan ever met his daughter?

Meanwhile, the shop still opened a couple of days a week, when the ferry came in, where Jake and Alva did their best to foist improbable souvenirs upon stray, unsuspecting tourists. And Jake realised one day that he'd never even noticed the change. The first two weeks on the island, he'd been a visitor himself – if not exactly a tourist, then an unwelcome arrival.

Now, he seemed to be part of the furniture, making bets about who'd be able to sell more of Duncan's tat – sorry, artisan, influencer-targeted, craft items. And sneaking the odd look at Alva, thinking each time – well, definitely cute, won't argue about that. Lovely? Debatable, still. But sweet? On him? Really?

She did seem to be less spiky with him recently, less prone to the death-stare, though she still had her moments. Understandable, really. He was amazed that she had managed to carry the entire secret on her own for so long.

"You never felt like telling anyone else?" he said, one afternoon.

"I told you – the General told you – " She dropped her voice when she mentioned his name, even in an empty shop on a quiet day. "It's too dangerous."

"Not even a friend? Someone you could really trust? Boyfriend, maybe?"

God, what did he say *that* for? That was Mrs Dunmore's fault, putting thoughts in his head.

"Fishing, are we?" Luckily, she looked amused.

"No, course not." He scrambled hastily. "Just, I thought, you know – "

"All right, Romeo, stop digging. No, no one. There isn't anyone on the island, anyway. Who would I tell? Bangkok Ewan? The man couldn't even climb on a bar without falling off."

"Fair point. Someone from university, maybe?"

"Yeah, well, you lose touch. Or they lose touch, with the girl who couldn't hack college and went back to live at home." Alva sounded – not bitter. Disappointed. Resigned.

"But that wasn't what happened?"

"What difference does it make? I decided to stay here, and I had to tell them something. What was I going to do? Call them up later – hey girlfriends, you'll never guess! I know! Teeny-tiny space fairies!"

"I suppose so."

"Anyway, they all graduated this year. The people I knew when I was there, I doubt they even remember me now."

Jake doubted that, in turn. There was something remarkable about Alva, the island girl who had traded in one future for another that couldn't yet be known. She'd gained something by choosing this life but had also lost things, for sure. Friends, a degree, a potential career.

There was something else he had been wondering about, too. Maybe something she could gain, rather than lose?

"You know the business with Ruan? I don't even know what to call it. With Eileen and the dancing?"

"It's some kind of memory-dive, prompted by the comms device." She tapped her ear. "It latches on to a picture you have in your mind, and the emotion you feel, and then projects it. Avatar tech. Not real, but not fake either. The Trogirans use it to stay in touch with their missing past – it makes them feel whole, they say. I think it helps Ruan – not to grieve exactly, but to remember that he was loved."

"What about you?" said Jake. This was encroaching on sticky ground, but she did seem to be more open to talking. To having a real conversation.

"What about me?"

"Have you done it, too? The memory-dive?"

"Me? Why?"

"I don't know, I thought – maybe, your mum? You could see her again."

The shutters went up immediately. Jake saw her eyes flash with annoyance.

"My mum?" said Alva. "She died when I was eight."

"I know, your dad said."

"Did he now? Well, he has his memories, but I don't remember her, not properly, I was too young. So, no, I haven't, and I'm not going to. All right?"

"Sure. Sorry."

Alva busied herself with some boxes in the shop, and Jake understood that the conversation was over, subject unwelcome. And he'd been shot down in flames, again.

But he did still wonder, because he didn't think that he would have forgotten about his mum if she had died when he was eight years old.

He had some very clear memories from that age – in the park one day with a kite, the games at a birthday party, the time he'd grazed his knee falling off his bike. He'd want to see her again, even if it was as a hologram – a ghostly projection from the past into the present. He'd want to feel those emotions, just for a minute or two, and couldn't understand who wouldn't?

Chapter 23

―――――――――

Now that he'd been accepted into the fold by the General, Jake was called upon more often to assist with things whenever he was up at the Strang house. Not just helping with the running of the place, but with what Jake thought of as "alien stuff."

He was still ordered around – the General finding it hard to shake his belief that, at heart, Jake was a mere servant – but at least they included him in the conversations now.

One day, the General had an unusual request – made from the video-comms screen before he and his accompanying crew emerged from the elevator chute.

"If I may be so bold, Lady Alva, we require the use of your surface vessel again. The boffins in the development lab have been working for quite some time on a quantum scanner to aid our search for the fleet. Infinitesimal odds, of course, given your planet's unfortunate location in this arm of the galaxy, far from the standard jump-lanes, but we must try our best."

Most of this washed over Jake, except for the two words he did recognise.

"We've got a surface vessel?"

"We've got a rowing boat." Alva indicated a battered, wooden craft, tied up on the other side of the boathouse. "Why do you need the boat, General?"

"Of course, it's beyond me, I'm just a simple starship captain" – some top humblebragging there – "but the boffins tell me that if we can raise a planet-side antenna, we may be able to boost the performance of the new scanning equipment."

"And the boat?"

"Ah, yes, that's the part I do understand. The antenna is too large for the transport elevator, so we'll be popping it out of the airlock shortly. If you wouldn't mind sending the Sassn– I mean, Jake, out in the vessel to retrieve it, then my chaps will be able to install the device promptly. Sergeant, prepare to beam us up!" And with that, the screen went blank and the chute began its countdown.

"You heard him," said Alva, amused. "In you get."

"No chance. I can't row that thing all the way out of the loch. Why can't you do it?"

"Oh no, the General wouldn't like that. I'm a lady, don't you know?"

"You're enjoying this. But seriously, I can't do that." Growing up by the coast, Jake had rowed a boat before. In a harbour, on a calm day, with a six-pack and a fishing rod. But heading miles out into deep Scottish waters to pick up a mystery package from a submerged spaceship, and then rowing all the way back? Not a chance.

The flashing countdown lights on the unit stopped and out popped the General, accompanied by two uniformed aides. A third crew member followed behind, with the requisite amount of facial hair but dressed in a flapping white tunic, with pale skin and rather wild eyes under a flyaway mop of bristled hair. Like a Trogiran Beaker.

"Now then, what's the delay?" The General was already strutting around. "You, sir, in the vessel at once! Science Officer Hvar here doesn't like to be out of the laboratory for long. Says the natural light is bad for his complexion – and I must say, you do look a bit peaky, Hvar." He lifted off and alighted on the bow of the rowing boat, which rocked slightly under his weight, and gestured at Jake to get in.

"He's just going now, General."

"I'm not."

As the General continued to harrumph, Alva was now openly laughing at Jake.

"Just get in," she said. "You big baby. You don't have to go miles out. They've done this before, you know? Shoot something out of the airlock with an attached propulsion unit, a tracer and a float. It'll pop up out there, about thirty feet from the boathouse," and she pointed out of the open side of the building, facing the water. "All right, Steve Redgrave, think you can manage that?"

"Is that thing even seaworthy?" Jake looked doubtfully at the boat. "I still think you should be doing it."

"A noble lady! The very thought!" The General had hopped back off the boat and was now hovering behind Jake, nudging and bumping him forwards in a flutter of wings. "Come on, sir, time is pressing. I thought you were here to assist us?"

"All right, all right." Jake clambered in and took the oars, while Alva cast him off, and he pulled slowly out into the loch.

Once in open water, thirty feet from the boathouse, he stopped to look around. He'd never seen the loch from this vantage point before. Ignoring the winged aliens inside the shelter, gesticulating and shouting, and a more-amused-than-she-should-be Alva, Jake had a glorious view of the bay, the beach, the glen behind, and the rising cliffs. There was barely a breeze, and he shipped the oars for a minute and trailed a hand in the water, wondering how long before the alien tech arrived.

There was more shouting from the boatshed, which he ignored. This was peaceful, and rather enjoyable. The General could wait.

He heard the noise first, before anything else – a low thrum, coming from behind him. He looked over his shoulder, and then turned the boat round awkwardly, to see a faint furrow in the water in the distance. This must be it.

The noise got louder, and although he couldn't see anything under the water, the agitation suggested something travelling at speed. The rowing boat began to rock slightly, and then more seriously, and Jake put the oars back in the water to try and regain some balance.

They've done this before. He just needed to sit tight and wait for the package to pop up, as promised. Haul it in the boat, row back, job done.

There was another shout from the boathouse, now behind him, which Jake was in no position to acknowledge, as he paddled his oars to steady the boat.

And then, with a roar and a drenching spray, a white sphere the size of a gym ball exploded from somewhere underneath the boat and tipped Jake into the water.

He surfaced, shocked and spluttering, and gripped the side of the rowing boat, as the wake subsided. Turned towards the boatshed, he watched the sphere – just a few feet away – bounce once or twice in the water and then come to a complete halt. It floated there, unmoving, and then began to move forward slowly, proceeding calmly towards the open side of the boathouse in what looked like a controlled, powered approach.

It took Jake two or three attempts to haul himself back into the boat, by which time the sphere had come to a rest inside the boathouse.

Shivering, even on a summer's day, he rowed himself back the thirty feet – freezing cold, soaked to the skin, water in his ears, nose running from the dunking. Alva was waiting for him, and pulled the line in, fastening it tight before standing back to let him climb out. He stood on the pier, dripping.

"I shouldn't laugh," she said. Laughing.

The two uniformed Trogirans stood above the white sphere, which sat on the water further down the pier, untethered but stationary. The top had been flipped open, so it now resembled two, hinged, half-spheres, and they were pulling out a shallow, parabolic dish about two feet in diameter. Science Officer Hvar buzzed around, making sure they handled it carefully, until it was laid safely on the pier, flat side down.

"Well?" said Jake, wringing out the bottom of his T-shirt. "I'm waiting."

"It's like this," said the General. "We did try and tell you, but you were deaf to our instructions. Perhaps next time, a little more attention to the task in hand?"

Alva stifled a giggle.

"You see, Science Officer Hvar was telling me that they have made some improvements to the delivery system. More accurate route-tracing, pin-point thrusters, stability gyros, that sort of thing. You'd have to ask him, I don't profess to understand it. Anyway, the long and short of it is, Lord Strang's surface vessel will no longer be required in such circumstances in the future. Although, of course, you should continue to exercise in the water as you see fit. I understand your species enjoys the experience?"

Full-blown snort from Alva. "Oh, come on," she said. "it's funny."

She found Jake an old towel from a metal locker, which smelled suspiciously of both oil and fish, and he patted himself down with it as much as he dared.

Meanwhile, the two Trogiran crew lifted the dish between them and fluttered up to the boathouse eaves, where they were joined by the science officer, tunic flapping as he directed its placement. A few bangs, whirs and clicks later, and they were all back on the pier, admiring their handiwork.

They had basically just installed a satellite dish in Ruan Strang's ramshackle boathouse, and the only saving grace was that – with any luck – it wouldn't be visible or recognisable from a passing boat out in the sound. Because that would be hard to explain.

The General seemed satisfied, though offered only a slender chance of success. "It's our duty to keep trying, of course, but the cosmos is a vast place. The boffins assure me that this antenna will assist their search for the fleet, but we have been disappointed before. Now, Lady Alva, shall we?"

He despatched the science officer back down the chute, who seemed relieved to be on his way, and accompanied Jake and Alva to the house. Jake squelched all the way back – he could hear his trainers squeaking on the track – and every time he sneaked a look at Alva, she seemed to be smiling.

Which was nice, but it still wasn't funny.

Chapter 24

A couple more weeks went by, with Jake firmly established in his new routine. In the shop twice a week with Alva. Trips down to meet the ferry for supplies. Up at Ruan's house two or three times a week, with occasional visits from the wee fellas.

It was all very domesticated – working, shopping, deliveries, household chores – provided your domestic situation also included wrangling beardy annoyances who thought they knew best.

Jake did what he was told by Alva – obviously – and didn't mind some direction by Ruan, whose house it was, after all. Not that Ruan seemed to mind what mess the house was in, as long as he could locate his whisky bottle and the TV remote.

But the General could, frankly, sod off. If the Trogirans were up at the house, he had a way of appearing without warning, hovering on silent wings behind Jake's shoulder and tapping with a scaly talon. Jake had almost had several heart attacks.

And, while Jake didn't know if it was a Trogiran thing, or a specifically General thing, he had an opinion about *everything*. The gist of which was that Jake was doing it wrong. Whatever it was.

Alva suggested he burn the excess packing boxes one day – all the chicken nugget packaging that had built up over the last couple of years. Jake liked the idea of that, and set off to build a fire in a paddock around the back of the house.

There was no chance, of course, that he be allowed to do that on his own, and the General had materialised to supervise – or interfere, depending on which side of the alien-human divide you came down upon.

"A conical structure would, of course, increase the air flow, but it's a matter for you."

"Je-sus! Don't do that. Can't you stick a bell on your wing or something?"

"I don't follow. That would alter the weight distrib-ution and disrupt the aerodynamic profile required to operate in this atmosphere, which the boffins assure me – "

"What do you want?" interrupted Jake, quickly stacking some sticks in a cone shape around a ball of paper.

"I was informed about this exercise and, technically, I should be the one to ignite the conflagration," said the General. "I do have executive authority in these matters. By the powers invested in me by the High Council, I should by rights – "

"I'm burning cardboard," said Jake. "It's not a high-level operation."

"Just as well," snorted the General. "Although a chap who can't operate a surface vessel without capsizing, is probably not the right sort for even this type of task."

He brought that up every time, too. Beardy and annoying.

Jake ignored that, crouched down to the paper and kindling, and took out a box of matches that he'd found in Ruan's kitchen.

"Yeah, well, it's my fire, and my planet," he said, striking a match, which failed to catch. He took another out of the box, which also failed. And another. Damp matches, typical. He'd have to go and look for another box, and he'd doubtless hear all about that, too.

"Allow me," said the General, who leaned forward with his lance.

"Jesus, not with that! You'll blow the whole house up."

The General tapped lightly on one side of the lance and a single spark caught a torn piece of cardboard, sending a flame curling up into the bonfire.

"It's the training, you see," said the General, stepping back in satisfaction. "Strang really will have to take you in hand."

Jake watched as half a dozen of the creatures tumbled around the boundaries of the fire, squawking in glee as the flames licked higher. Just like kids, or indeed human male adults, any time there was a fire to be lit and a debate to be had about who was in charge.

If he wasn't up at the Strang house, Jake was down at Castle View, working on the property. At least here, Duncan let him get on with things on his own, and he enjoyed the freedom and the sense of achievement.

He painted the downstairs reception rooms in the main house, and tidied up the lawns and garden at the front as best he could. Took the weeds out of the gravel driveway, cleaned the front-facing windows – those not boarded up – and scrubbed and whitewashed the main steps. Pretty impressive, though he said so himself, when he stood back to look.

"Nice work," said Duncan, when he saw the progress. To Jake's surprise, he even opened his wallet. "How long has that taken you? A day or so?"

"Four days, total," said Jake firmly.

"Two it is then." Duncan handed him another sixty quid. When Jake looked at him questioningly, he added, "You'll have had your meals, of course."

"And my comfortable live-in accommodation," said Jake, but Duncan affected not to notice.

He took some new photographs of the façade and driveway for the estate agent, who had promised to come and do it himself but had never materialised.

"Hard to sell, he reckons, in the current climate," said Duncan. "I don't think he's even trying. But it's scrubbed up nicely. These photos should raise a bit of interest."

Jake wasn't sure about that. After all his work, the building looked fine as far as the front door, but inside – and especially upstairs – there was an awful lot to do to bring it back to life.

The bathrooms required a complete refurbishment, the window frames were rotting, floorboards needed replacing, and there were dangling wires and cracked pipes in every room. Those were just the things that Jake could see were wrong. Any surveyor or builder was going to be doing a lot of lip-pursing and dismissive whistling. Even if someone cut the trees down and miraculously restored the view of the castle, he couldn't see anyone wanting to buy the Castle View in its current state.

Duncan seemed happy though, and forwarded the photos, and Jake went around the rear to the outbuildings to see if he could find a rake for the mossy lawn.

When he came back, Duncan was finishing up a phone call. "Great!" he said. "I'll meet you off the ferry. See you then."

Jake had never seen him so happy. Probably snagged a deal on a consignment of hand-painted Bulgarian water-bottles.

"You'll never guess. That was the estate agent. Seems my email prompted a call. He's coming over, he's got a proposal to make. An offer."

Chapter 25

Duncan sent Jake down to the ferry to meet the agent.

"Just need to finalise some numbers," he said. "Check my position, that sort of thing," like he was about to unload pork belly futures rather than try to sell a dilapidated activity centre. "His name's Armstrong. Bring him to the office" – meaning the hotel – "and we'll have a quiet chat there."

Jake took Duncan's van, drove down to the ferry, and picked up a guy in a tailored grey suit wearing black brogues and Ray-Bans, which immediately made him the best-dressed man on Elsay.

Armstrong remained tight-lipped on the drive up to the village, aside from a few comments about the length of the crossing. Jake got the impression he was a little out of his comfort zone, though he could count himself lucky – at least he hadn't had to wait for a non-existent bus.

At the edge of the village, as they passed the

entrance to Castle View, Jake slowed a little and pointed it out.

"Mr Fraser will take you down later," he said. "He's up at the hotel now. Couple of minutes away."

"The hotel, right," said Armstrong. "Good."

Jake stopped on the quayside, outside the hotel, and the agent got out. Jake pointed at the front door, before indicating that he was going to park the van around the side, and the guy nodded, but walked to the edge of the quay first. Got out his phone, snapped a few shots of the harbour, then turned around and framed the hotel, too. Seemed satisfied and walked in through the door to the bar.

Jake followed a couple of minutes later to find that the agent was already getting the full Duncan Fraser treatment. Admittedly, he was good at this sort of stuff – smoothing over, softening up. Whatever the agent had to say was about to come up against the swirling tide of Duncan's boundless optimism.

"Mr Armstrong, Steven, isn't it? Can I call you Steven? Here, have a pew. Jimmy, a drink for Steven. Not the Beserker, a proper drink."

Jimmy went straight to the top-shelf whisky, which was unheard of, but the agent stopped him with a raised hand.

"A glass of water will be fine," he said.

Jimmy looked perplexed, like he'd never heard of the drink.

"Bottled, you mean? Mineral water, is that it? Not much call for it, round here." He filled a wine glass from the sink tap, added a slice of lemon, made a 'What-can-I-do?' face at Duncan and delivered the drink.

"Now, Mr Fraser," said Armstrong the agent. "It's like this."

"Yes?" said Fraser, clasping his hands together. Jake wouldn't put it past him to roll out a prayer mat and supplicate himself entirely, this close to a deal.

"As you know, as well as the usual day-to-day business at the agency, I represent some rather more select clients. International clients, you might say. Looking for investment opportunities."

"I remember, I remember," said Duncan. "Of course, investment opportunity, makes sense." He took a large gulp from his usual tumbler of red wine and nodded seriously.

Behind the bar, Jimmy raised his eyebrows at Jake and mumbled, "He can smell the money, you see? Always had the nose for it, has Duncan."

"And I've been instructed by one of my clients to sound out a property on the island. Perfect for what they have in mind. Ideal location, singular building, ripe for boutique development." Armstrong tapped the table in emphasis.

Duncan couldn't help himself, restraint all gone.

"I've always said so, Steven. Just needs a bit of vision. And investment, as you say – but international clients, they'd know all about that. I tried, and I made a good go of it, although I say so myself. But it's time to let someone else take the reins. I'll be sorry to see it go, of course, but the Castle View will rise again, I'm sure, under the right owners. May I ask what the offer is?"

Armstrong looked puzzled, and if he noticed that Duncan was almost fizzing with excitement, he didn't show it.

"Castle View?" he said.

"The activity centre," clarified Duncan. "And you telling me it would be hard to sell." He waggled a finger at Armstrong. "House and grounds like that, solid bones, plenty of space, I'm surprised it's taken you this long to rustle up a buyer. Still, all's well in the end, wouldn't you say? Jimmy, another wine, when you're ready, and another, erm, water for young Steven here."

"Oh, dear me, no," said Armstrong.

"Excellent, a celebration it is. A wee dram for the man instead, James. No, make that a large dram."

"I mean no to the activity centre," said Armstrong. "Castle View? That old place? We've had no interest in that. Not for over a year now. As I've mentioned before, I think you're going to find that very hard to sell in the current climate."

Duncan's face fell. Jake had never seen a man so deflated, so quickly.

"I don't understand," he said, with the tone of a man who'd excitedly opened a tin of Quality Street to find there were only the blue coconut ones left.

"Extremely hard," said Armstrong, warming to his subject. "If not impossible. In the existing climate, at this moment in time."

"All right," said Duncan. "No need to rub it in.

Then I don't understand. Who's your client? What do they want?"

"They have a portfolio of exclusive hotels around the world. Several here in Scotland, in the high-end leisure market. You'll remember their interest last year in the Strang property? Well, they'd like to revisit – "

"Not this again," said Duncan, downing the rest of his wine and signalling to the bar for another. His dejection appeared complete. No one was coming to buy Castle View.

Standing in the background, Jake had his own concerns, seeing that his only real source of income – preparing the activity centre for a possible sale – was now almost certainly going to dry up.

"I think you'll be – "

Duncan shushed Armstrong with a hand. "Look, it's hopeless, we tried last time. Ruan Strang doesn't want to sell and no one can make him. And my daughter has strong views on the subject, too, so – "

"I remember," said Armstrong. "A colourful turn of phrase, I recall. Quite the wordsmith."

"She's a strong-willed girl, what can I say? And Strang won't have changed his mind. Anyway, you've had a wasted journey, I'm sorry. But you should have said on the phone, instead of getting up a man's hopes."

"You misunderstand me, Mr Fraser. It's not the Strang property I'm here about. My clients have moved on from that, they understand the situation. But they love the island and its potential. They have their eye on a smaller property – a much more realistic target, they feel, and one which would fit their boutique portfolio."

Armstrong mentioned the names of new, small-scale, designer hotels in Oban and Ullapool, and talked of the visitor potential in what he called the island-urban interface, where creatives and business strivers met the authentic face of an ancient culture.

Duncan looked confused.

"I had to come and see for myself, at their behest," said Armstrong, "and now that I'm here, I can see it's perfect. A wonderful location. It's far from a wasted journey, Mr Fraser. In fact, it was you yourself who alerted me to the possibility, when we first talked, a couple of years ago. You have an interest in the hotel, I believe you told me? And this, I take it, is your business partner?" He indicated Jimmy.

Probably because Jake didn't have a financial interest in any of this, he was way ahead of the other two, who were still casting looks at each other, trying to work out exactly which property Armstrong was talking about.

"My clients would like to buy the hotel, Mr Fraser," said Armstrong, finally putting them out of their misery. "They're offering 800,000 pounds, though I think they might be prepared to go a little higher."

"What?" said Duncan and Jimmy, simultaneously. Their faces lit up.

Jake had never seen expressions change so completely and rapidly. Like they'd rustled among the discarded wrappers and discovered a toffee finger. Not one to share between them. A toffee finger *each*. An unimaginable surprise.

Jake felt a presence by his side, and another exclamation, though the tone was markedly different.

"What?" said Alva, fixing all three men with a DEFCON 1 stare.

Chapter 26

By the time Jake had got back from dropping the estate agent at the ferry – as the only one sober enough to drive – the party at the hotel was in full swing.

The doors to the bar were wide open, as people spilled out into the heat of an early July afternoon. Jimmy was dispensing bottom-shelf whisky and pints of Berserker like there was no tomorrow – which was a distinct possibility for the more overly refreshed villagers, tottering on the edge of the quayside, oblivious of the drop to the water below.

Duncan, meanwhile, was brandishing a brochure left by the agent, and holding forth about the projected benefits of the island-urban interface as represented by the soon-to-be-acquired Port Hotel. If he couldn't fully explain what 'boutique' meant, as far as the hotel's future was concerned, he was on firmer ground about what it would mean for Elsay.

"Tourists," he proclaimed. "Visitors. Jobs. Money."

"They'll be wanting grapefruit mineral water," growled Jimmy. "Raspberry hibiscus kombucha. Craft gin."

"Wee plates of tapas. Heritage carrots. Lobster foam."

There was a momentary silence as they pondered the implications, before a buoyant shout of "Ker-ching!"

A roar went up as Bangkok Ewan climbed onto the bar and then fell backwards into waiting arms, before being crowd-surfed out through the door and tipped into the harbour. He surfaced to chants of "Bang-kok, Bang-kok!" as, for once, everyone dropped the pretence that he didn't know they called him that. In turn, Bangkok splashed to the harbour ladder, hauled himself out and accepted the public adulation, whipping up the chant before throwing himself in again.

Jake looked for Alva but she was nowhere to be found. Unsurprising, really, if her demeanour at the news was anything to go by. Also unsurprisingly, Duncan hadn't noticed Alva's absence, taking her exclamation to be in the same vein as his – shock, surprise, delight.

But this was the Strang offer all over again for Alva. Concern at the prospect of an inundation of new visitors to the island; the fear of discovery; the end of her – their – secret.

And, worse, there wasn't going to be anything she could do to stall this one. It was what Duncan – Jimmy, the island – had been waiting for. A lifeline.

Jake felt conflicted but accepted a couple of free drinks from the bar – never knew when that might happen again – before slipping away. It didn't feel right, joining in with the celebrations, given what was at stake.

He was going to go up to Ruan's place the next day, Sunday, to see if Alva was there, but thought he'd give her some space.

He poked his head into the bar instead in the afternoon, to see the lie of the land, and a deathly, stale silence filled the air. It looked like the aftermath of a precision strike by a guided missile. As he stepped through the threshold, empty bottles skittled across the carpet.

Jake had once been to an 'upside-down' bar in Berlin where the furniture was fixed to the ceiling, and the lights and chandeliers sprouted from the floor. Jimmy had clearly been, too, and had taken notes, though he'd added his own, freestyle ideas. There was one solitary shoe on the counter, another – from a different pair – fastened with a dart to the dartboard, and a pile of empty beer cans in one corner so deep it looked like a play-pit for alcoholics. The clean-up would be monumental.

With nothing better to do on the Monday, Jake made his way back to the hotel. Surprisingly, the bar was now in a semblance of order and smelled strongly of pine disinfectant. You still couldn't describe it as having a boutique ambience, but you would no longer be duty bound to notify the local health and safety executive.

Duncan was there, looking business-like, tapping away at his iPad.

"Just the man!" he said, which was generally the prelude to getting Jake to do something strenuous for little or no pay. "Very exciting news about the hotel, isn't it? I'll need you up a ladder later this week, see if we can't clean those gutters."

And there it was. Jake particularly liked the 'We.'

But there was more, and it was something of a surprise.

"Come up to the house tomorrow night?" said Duncan. "Family dinner. What do you say?"

Jake tried to unpick this.

"Your house, you mean? Not the hotel?"

"Absolutely. Thought it would be nice to have a chat about things."

"Things?"

"Business things. You've got a sensible head on you, Jake. You understand how the world works. Nice chat, family meal, are you in?"

"Family? You mean Alva? She'll be there?"

"Well, it's her house, too, Jake." Duncan brushed off the question with a smile. "And what with you two getting on so well, I thought, maybe a pleasant family meal together, you know…"

Jake blanched at the implied familiarity, and glanced nervously over to the bar, but Jimmy wasn't there to hear.

"Well…"

"That's the spirit. Shall we say seven o'clock? Good man."

Before he'd had time to think up an excuse, Jake had been bounced into it.

It's not that he wasn't curious about Duncan's house – Alva's home, on the hill up towards the castle. He'd been on the island over a month, and he'd never been invited before. He'd certainly never thought of calling up there on the off chance, to see if Alva was around. She kept that part of her life private and Jake hadn't pried. He saw her in neutral places – the shop, the hotel, Ruan's place – and he assumed that's how she wanted it.

Yet, while it was an opportunity to find out more about Alva, he had a shrewd idea that this suggestion was nothing to do with Duncan wanting to play happy families.

If Jake had to bet, he was sure that Alva had been giving her dad the full and unexpurgated version of her treatise on 'Why selling the hotel to outside investors is a truly terrible idea.' There was probably a flip-chart presentation and a bulleted information sheet. Duncan's ears had doubtless been bent out of shape over the last thirty-six hours, and this was another truly terrible idea of his to persuade her otherwise.

Business matters? He knew how the world works? Please, it was a naked attempt to enlist Jake's help, based on the zero-evidence premise that his, Duncan's, daughter had feelings for the island's largely unpaid day labourer.

Duncan was up from his seat and heading for the door when Jimmy came back into the bar.

"Right, Jimmy, I'm off," he said. "The lad's coming up to the house for dinner tomorrow night. You know?" and he nodded meaningfully.

Oh, god, don't tell Jimmy.

"Sort him out a bottle, will you?" said Duncan, on his way out of the door.

Jimmy reached down behind the bar. "He does like the old Rioja," he said. "The 2018 is a lovely drop. Take him this."

Jake accepted the bottle. "Thanks very much." Maybe there were some benefits to knowing the joint owners of an upcoming boutique island hotel with an urban twist?

"Thirty-five quid," said Jimmy, "I'll put it on your tab."

———————

Chapter 27

———————

The following evening, Jake walked up to the Fraser house in bright sunshine, taking big strides up the hillside road that curled around to the castle above.

He enjoyed the feeling of the sun on his neck, even at this hour. The long days and short nights agreed with him.

At first, he had thought he wouldn't be able to sleep – with the sun setting at almost eleven pm and rising again well before four – but it was quite the opposite. He fell asleep most nights the minute his head hit the pillow, and slept like a gangly, 22-year-old baby. Must be all the work and exercise.

He hadn't seen Alva since Saturday night, and the news about the hotel, but as he rang the doorbell he could hear her voice ringing through the house. In her natural habitat, shouting her head off, like a herder calling in the yaks across the steppes.

"Not now, dinner's ready! Whoever it is, get rid of them till later."

Duncan opened the door. A bit sheepish.

"She doesn't know I'm coming?" Somehow, this was no surprise.

"Lovely treat for her. Come on in. The Rioja? You shouldn't have."

The house was one of those nineteenth-century Scottish island villas that thinks it's on Capri, with a couple of turrets and balconies, a stone terrace and cascading gardens. Fine for Capri, of course. More challenging, no doubt, in a Hebridean winter, though the midsummer evening light was showing it at its best.

The sun caught the colours in a stained-glass window above the door, as he stepped into a spacious lobby with a tiled floor, an old church pew on one side and a row of brass coat hooks on the other.

Duncan led him through the house into a lounge room with high, deep windows overlooking the harbour far below. Jake could make out the roof of the hotel and the curve of the cottages. There was a pair of binoculars on a window seat, next to an open astronomy book, and Jake wondered if Alva had been scanning the night skies, looking for Trogir and the Kotor System?

Duncan touched his arm and pointed behind him, where a large arch led through to an adjacent farm-house kitchen-diner at the rear of the house.

"Look who I've found," said Duncan.

"What are you doing here?" said Alva.

And the pleasant family evening was off to a terrific start.

"Sit down, Jake, sit down," said Duncan, pointing at a sofa. "I invited the lad. Thought it might be nice. Show him some island hospitality."

"Did you now?" said Alva, getting in one of her stock phrases early.

"You always cook plenty of food," said Duncan.

"Yes, I *always* cook," said Alva.

"Ah, now, darling, let's not have that. Sit yourself down here, Jake, come on."

Jake found himself mouthing "Sorry" at Alva, while she did her "Don't-darling-me" routine with Duncan. All the greatest hits.

While Alva clattered around in the kitchen – possibly more than strictly necessary – Jake took in the room. It was cosier than Strang's place – the only other private house he'd been in on Elsay – and more stylish, too. Furnished in this century, anyhow, with a brighter décor of pastel colours and painted pine furniture. There was a large TV on one wall, and an open cube shelving unit with piles of design and garden books, interspersed with tasteful ceramics that had definitely not been made by the island's artisan stone-painter.

Photographs were staggered at angles along a low, cream sideboard – a wedding picture, clearly of Duncan and, presumably, the new Mrs Fraser; Alva as a baby, scowling, obviously; and a separate one of a bright, athletic-looking, blonde woman with tied-back hair.

"Swedish," said Fraser, noticing Jake looking around. The décor or Mrs F, it wasn't quite clear, until he said, "Anja, Alva's mum, bless her."

The atmosphere improved with the arrival of the food – baked fillets of hake, potato wedges, green salad – and the real-time proof, by Duncan, that red wine went very nicely with fish. "Stick it in the fridge for twenty minutes, Jakey boy, don't let the snobs tell you otherwise," he said.

Jake wasn't much of a one for wine, although now he knew that the stuff Duncan drank cost over thirty quid a bottle, he figured he'd get some of his missing wages back by knocking back a glass or two. He couldn't say that he enjoyed it particularly, but that wasn't the point, and it least it wasn't Little Widdle.

"Haven't seen you around?" he said Alva, trying to make conversation. "I've missed you. Well, you know, not 'missed you' missed you. Must have missed you, I mean, when I was looking for you."

Jake could hear how pathetic that sounded before he got anywhere near the end of the sentence. Alva had her eyebrows raised, accompanied by a vaguely amused but pained look that gave him no encouragement at all. He gave up and pushed a potato wedge around his plate.

Duncan watched on, looking pleased, like part one of his cunning plan was all coming together. Alva said, "Well, a lot's been happening," but didn't elaborate, and because Duncan was Duncan and couldn't help himself, he took this as invitation to launch part two.

"Of course, darling. Big news about the hotel. It's a lot to take in. Could change everything for us. Jake here was only telling me yesterday that it's all very exciting."

Alva's head jerked up, eyes popping, like she'd been sprung from a jack-in-the-box. She fixed Jake with a look that said, "Oh yes, buster?" and replaced the faint air of amusement with the gimlet-eyed glare of a magistrate considering a lengthy custodial sentence as a deterrent against littering.

Jake could see now why the phrase "Bloody Duncan" got a lot of use on the island. He'd just been thrown under a bus in return for a portion of hake and a glass of lightly chilled red wine.

"I don't think I said that, exactly." He hadn't said it at all, but now he was firmly in the middle of two Frasers, one conniving, one cute, both dangerous in their own way.

"Alva's worried about change coming to the island," said Duncan, determined to press the point. "Aren't you, darling? Thinks a new development might be too much. Might change the character of Port Levin. And we do have to take that into consideration, we really do. But it's like you said, Jake – "

Bloody, bloody Duncan.

"We shouldn't be afraid of change. Look at you. Come up here from England, all on your own, no job, no money –"

A bit rich, whose fault was that?

"Yet here you are, helping me – us – change Elsay for the better. New opportunities, new friends. See,

Alva, not all change is bad. You'd never have met young Jake here otherwise, that's all I'm saying. And now I'm going outside for a constitutional, let you pair of lovebirds have a nice little chat."

Duncan threw open a French door, stepped onto the terrace and disappeared down into the garden, having driven the bus backwards and forwards over Jake's lifeless body before erecting a bus-shaped monument over his grave and signalling a 21-bus salute.

There was a long silence. Jake wasn't even going to address the 'lovebirds' business. Head down, hope it went away. In the end, he just said, "Constitutional?"

"It's what he calls having a whisky in the garden. He's got a bottle under the bird bath."

"You know I didn't say any of those things?"

"I figured. Bloody Duncan. I knew he was up to something. Suppose he thinks you can persuade me."

"I figured. Bloody Duncan."

They both sat there for a few seconds, until Jake said, "Where have you been? I *have* been looking for you."

That was it, that was the word. *Looking* for you, not *missing* you. Idiot.

"Where do you think? Trying to talk to my ridiculous father, who thinks all his birthdays have come at once. I know what he's like. He'll have spent the money before it even arrives, and he'll be busy roping others into new ventures. I thought I might be able to appeal to his sense of culture and tradition, but the problem with that is – "

"He doesn't have one."

"Exactly. He's going to take the money, him and Jimmy, and they're going to open the island up. And I don't know what to do about it."

For the first time since he'd known her, Alva looked beaten. Diminished. Frightened, even. "They're going to be discovered. The Trogirans. It's only a matter of time."

"Maybe not?" said Jake. "It might not happen. They must be looking at other properties, too."

"The agent seemed fairly certain that it would. They'd have bought Ruan's place last year, if they could. This time, there's nothing to stop them buying the hotel."

"Then perhaps it won't be so bad? No one can still go on Strang's land if he doesn't want them. And we can keep them hidden, get them to stay on the ship for longer. Who's to say anything would change?"

Alva screwed her eyes tight before replying – dismissing Jake's vague hopes.

"He's already mentioned going up to see Ruan, trying to talk him around, get access to the beach again. The agent mentioned consulting a solicitor, to see if there's anything they can do about the road. And look – you found your way there eventually. There's only one of you. What about when there's a team of contractors here for months on end? Or a hotel full of wandering guests looking for that perfect Instagram shot?"

It poured out of her. And while she was clearly fearing the worst, these were all good points. The sale might not happen at all, but now that the offer had been made, the risk to the aliens was higher than it had ever been since their arrival.

"And can you imagine the sideshow that Duncan will put on, if he finds out there are visitors from space? He'll be selling teas to MI5, or whoever they send up here to take them away. Printing commemorative certificates."

"We could neutralise him?" Jake said it as a joke, hoping to lighten the mood.

"Well, we need to do something," said Alva, which wasn't a total repudiation of the potential liquidation of her father. "We're going to have to talk to the Trogi-rans. Tell them what's going on."

Chapter 28

"Tell me again about this 'estate agent'?" said the General, singling out the unfamiliar words. "Sounds like an absolute blighter."

They were holding an emergency meeting under cover in the boatshed. Not at the house, at Alva's insistence, to be on the safe side. Knowing there was now an offer to buy the hotel had added an extra layer of caution, and Jake, Ruan and Alva had felt unseen eyes on them as they had made their way down the glen and across the beach to the pier.

The General had arrived with three of his most trusted lieutenants, and all were perched on the metal storage boxes lining one side of the boatshed.

"Armstrong," said Ruan. "Wee bastard tried to buy me out last year. Doesn't give up."

"Not one of your countrymen, Lord Strang? Sassnack, I suppose? Devious? Underhand? Yes, it all makes sense."

This was water off a duck's back to Jake by now, but he did idly consider whether he should stand up for his home nation a bit more. If the Trogirans ever departed, with stories of their exile, the reputation of the English across the galaxy would be mud. The Scots, on the other hand, would probably be feted in every star system between here and Alpha Canis Majoris.

"I think we should restrict visits to the house," said Alva. "At least until I can find out a little more about what's going on."

There was a flutter of wings and an undercurrent of chatter among the lieutenants, one of whom leaned into the General's ear.

"I'm only thinking of your safety," said Alva.

"Well, of course, Lady Alva, though the chaps are a little concerned that they'll miss the forthcoming nuptials of Mary and Adam on the prairie. It's a testing time for all."

Not for the first time, Jake wondered what grasp on reality the Trogirans had. They had mastered trans-galactic travel and seen the planet Earth as they'd approached – presumably recorded its size, physical aspect and geographical variation? Must have noticed its level of technology, and intercepted its communications and transmissions?

Yet they seemed to think films and TV shows were documentaries, and that Ruan Strang's little empire was representative of the entire planet.

Or they were messing with the earthlings, like a

gang of aliens in the *Men in Black* arrivals hall. That could always be it.

The General was still musing on the information he'd been given. "If this impertinent fellow, Agent Armstrong, succeeds in his endeavour, there will be an influx of outsiders with strange ways on Lord Strang's land?"

Close enough.

"Outsiders who would put our way of life at risk? Endanger our presence here?"

Again, close enough.

"I'll not let them find you," said Ruan. "You need have no fear." He had drawn himself up to his full height. Sober, determined. Taking his role as Lord Protector seriously – only slightly undermined by his general appearance, looking more like a man who'd recently spent six months digging drainage ditches in the Cairngorms than a noble ally in a just cause.

"Your service is never in doubt, Lord Strang. You are a true friend to the Trogirans."

Ruan saluted the General. This meant something to him, it was clear to see.

"And – forgive me, Lady Alva, I know it must be a painful subject – but your father is facilitating this outrage? Consorting with this Agent Armstrong for his own personal gain?"

They had tried to explain to the General about property and land ownership, but he didn't seem to understand that Ruan couldn't simply forbid the hotel purchase. Or have Duncan and Jimmy strapped to a table and subjected to something he referred to as 'neural cleansing.'

"Would that hurt much?" Alva had asked, considering all options. But gratifying as it was to think of, Jake moved the discussion on.

"Practically, what does it all mean? Even if they do sell it?" he said. "Nothing's going to happen straight away. It takes ages to sort out a sale. I'm not sure there's anything we can do right now, except wait and see what happens. And take extra care to keep you hidden, of course."

"If we must stay on the vessel for now, then we must," said the General. "If it was just us chaps, we could organise and fight – "

"That's a terrible idea."

"Put the blasters up him, sir!"

"Give this Agent Armstrong a taste of Trogiran metal!"

"No one is putting anything up anyone. He's an estate agent. They'd only be another one along, even if you managed to get rid of this one."

"Self-replicating, eh? Able to spawn at will? Tricky blighters, these estate agents, I thought as much. Still, as I said, I'm afraid taking the fight to the enemy is not an option. I have the safety of the vessel to consider. The rest of the crew, the chaps in the cryo-chambers – I must do everything in my power to protect them. We shall lie low for now and await your advice. You know the ways of this Agent Armstrong, I assume? You will be able to thwart him?"

"Wee bastard," said Ruan. "Wouldn't trust him as far as I could kick him. He comes anywhere near my land, I'll see him off, don't you worry."

Yet another concern to manage. It was bad enough that there was a ship-full of gung-ho gremlins itching to notch an estate-agent kill. It only needed Ruan Strang to wade in with his shotgun and they'd all be sunk.

And of the two scenarios, that was far the more likely. The Trogirans had a vested interest in staying hidden. The last thing they wanted was news of an alien landing blasted around the planet's airwaves. If the Niksic were watching and listening, their very survival would be at stake.

Ruan would have to be made to understand. The less attention they all drew to themselves, the safer his wee pals would be.

"And now that's settled," said the General, with a slight flutter of his wings, "let's consider the ongoing proceedings at the house on the prairie. I think a regular update for my chaps should do the trick. Lord Strang, if you wouldn't mind despatching the Sassnack to the comms module whenever there have been developments" – he tapped the chute's screen with a claw – "I'll ensure the news is disseminated among the crew."

Chapter 29

As predicted, Jake spent much of the following week up
a ladder at the Port Hotel. Duncan still had hopes of
being able to sell Castle View, possibly even to the same
investors, but for now all work was to be diverted into
sprucing up the hotel. All hands on deck, was the cry.
Jake's hands, obviously.

Jake could hardly refuse if he wanted to stay on the
island. And he knew now that he wanted to stay – more
than anything. However this turned out, he wanted to
be a part of it. He wanted to know what happened
next. Who wouldn't?

Duncan made it even easier, because – pound signs
dancing in front of his eyes – he paid Jake two
hundred quid up front, cash in hand. And gave him a
new boss.

"This is Dougie," he said, introducing a small,
elderly gent in blue overalls and a knitted cap, with skin
like a papyrus scroll found in a desert cave. "What he

doesn't know about painting and decorating isn't worth knowing. Right, Dougie?"

Dougie muttered a sentence or two that was entirely unintelligible, handed Jake some sandpaper and pointed him up the ladder to a first-floor window.

"That's it," said Duncan. "Good one, Dougie, always with the jokes."

For the rest of the morning, Jake sanded window frames from the top of a precarious ladder, moving slowly along the front of the hotel under Dougie's direction.

Not that Jake could understand anything that Dougie said.

There were occasional words in there that he recognised – "Up. Ladder. Jesus. Useless." – and others that sounded as though he should understand their meaning – "Bawbag. Spanner. Dolly. Mince." – but couldn't see how they applied to the painting of a dilapidated harbour hotel. It was like being ordered around by a leathery Billy Connolly in paint-spattered dungarees, and not getting any of the punchlines.

What Dougie knew about painting and decorating never became clear, because he never actually did any, dividing his time between shouting up unintelligible instructions and gazing out across the harbour. Occasionally, for variety, he would launch a pebble at a seagull. Then, at precisely noon every day, Dougie would let go of the ladder and totter off inside the hotel bar.

"Wee swally," he'd announce, mysteriously, before disappearing, usually for the rest of the day. Leaving

Jake to try and determine how to apply his other departing words – "Pish. Bampot. Glaikit. Rocket." – to the sanding and painting of a weatherworn window frame.

"Got you up there, has he? How much is he paying you?"

Jake looked down to see Bangkok Ewan, who gave the ladder a not unfriendly shake.

"Two hundred this time."

Bangkok whistled. "Rather you than me."

Jake climbed down and looked back up at the hotel façade. Four first-floor windows on either side of the main entrance. Eight frames to sand and paint in all. This was the third day and he'd done half of them already.

"I thought that was pretty good?"

"You know there's four sides to the building, right? And the conservatory dining room?"

"He never mentioned anything about that."

Bangkok roared with laughter and wiped an eye. Shook his head at Jake, like – you'll never learn.

"I hear he's got old Dougie with you? Where is he?"

"Inside," said Jake. "Looking for a wee swally, whatever that is. He never seems to find one."

Bangkok made a rapid drinking gesture. "That's him done for the day. He'll be lying down in the back room with a bottle, watching *Homes Under the Hammer*. You'll be getting on with him all right, though? Chatting away?"

Not exactly. Jake got the drift of what Dougie was

telling him, but only after much finger-pointing, gesticulating and operatic throat-clearing. Not Dougie's fault, but Jake had never encountered such a strong Scottish accent before. It was embarrassing how little he understood of what Dougie said, given they were supposed to be speaking the same language.

"I don't understand him, to be honest. I know that's my problem. I find his accent hard to follow. Don't get half of what he says."

"Really?" Bangkok looked surprised.

"What, and you do?"

"Ah well, fair play, he's always been a bit hard to understand. But then, so are you sometimes."

"I am?" Jake hadn't given much thought to this until now. He had an accent, he knew that. Everyone did. But he'd just supposed that, even though he was in Scotland, he was speaking English to people who spoke English. What he hadn't fully appreciated was that Scotland wasn't, in fact, England. Despite all the clues. Not the same country at all, it turned out. Maybe that did make him hard to understand? Or maybe it just made him English and clueless.

"Ah, you're fine," said Bangkok. "You're nothing like old Dougie Crowther, that's for sure."

"Crowther? Dougie's a Crowther?"

One of the infamous Crowthers with a bit of English in them? Jake had heard them mentioned many times, usually when he was being misidentified as a long-lost family member. Up until now, he'd not encountered a Crowther, having assumed they'd all been run off by pitchfork-wielding islanders at some point in the past.

"Aye, that's them. One of the family went down south, married an English lass. The shame of it killed his parents."

Jake was struggling to keep up, still trying to match the picture he had in his head of an island Crowther with a bit of English in him and the evidence of the impenetrable, beery, painter and decorator.

"Dougie married an English girl? And his parents killed themselves?" That sounded extreme, even for a place that had experienced a tsunami and an alien landing in the last few years.

"Dougie? No, this was back in the 1850s. Dougie's great-great-great something or other. Thought they'd married up in the world. Got themselves airs and graces. Notions. Well, you've heard him talk, you'll know."

"He doesn't sound anything like an English person! I don't even think that's English he's speaking."

"Ah, well, no. As I said, the shame of it. Couldn't stay in England, couldn't come back to the island, so after a few months they went to Glasgow by all accounts."

"Dougie's great-great-great grandparents did? In the 1850s?"

"That's it. They've always been a bit different, the Crowthers. It's the English in them. You don't hear it?"

Jake looked at Bangkok. Straight-faced, not a hint of a raised eyebrow or anything else that might signify a joke. He'd been here several weeks now, and Jake was still waiting for the day – the one conversation – when someone would say something completely implausibly, like this, wait for Jake to take the bait, and then go "Aaaaah, gotcha!"

Not today, apparently.

"I don't hear it," he said. A Crowther many generations ago had once spent ten minutes in England, and Jake was supposed to spot layers of King Charles under Frankie Boyle?

"Ah well," said Bangkok, "Maybe not your part of England. Anyway, you crack on, I've got to go and see Duncan about where exactly he wants this drone."

Jake had one foot on the ladder. "Drone?"

"The wee flying thing."

"I know what a drone is. What's Duncan want one for?"

"Fly one up and down the coast. Promotional video. Thinks he can get the price up if he shows them the lie of the land. Cliffs, heather, beaches, you know? Eagle's eye view of bonnie old Scotland."

That didn't sound good.

"You've got a drone?" This was less of a surprise than it might have been. Everyone on Elsay seemed to have multiple jobs. Why would the guitarist-handyman be any different?

"Certainly have," said Bangkok, producing a business card. "Full licence, too. It's in the van. No wind this afternoon, good time for it."

Jake turned the card over in his hand.

Ewan Robertson: Axe-Shredder, Creative Artisan (Domestic and Corporate), Drone Pilot.

"4K, 360-degree mode, anti-coll sensors, 5km transmission," said Bangkok.

Jake supposed all that meant something.

"She's a beauty. Get her over the cliffs, into the loch and along the bays, no trouble. Close up, see everything."

Oh right, that did mean something. That meant…

Oh.

Bollocks.

Chapter 30

"Ewan, good man." Duncan had come out of the hotel. "You got it?"

"In the van, chief." Bangkok nodded at the battered old Transit on the quayside, emblazoned with a logo of a duelling electric guitar and power drill.

"Drone footage, Jake, my boy," said Duncan. "All the rage. You should have a look at Ewan's YouTube. All those aerial views of Thailand. Bangkok, was it now?" Fraser winked at Jake.

"Pattaya, I've told you a million times."

"Aye, Pattaya, that's it. Anyway, let's get you set up."

Jake followed them to the van, where Bangkok opened the rear doors and began assembling his kit. He loaded everything into a big, double-handled holdall, which went over his shoulders, on his back.

"Good lad," said Duncan. "Up the path behind the hotel, onto the top there. Grand day for it. You'll get some beautiful shots of the loch. The pier, old Strang's boathouse, the beach – it'll look a picture. And then up for a sweep over the water from on high. Lovely and clear on a day like today."

"It's barely a path," said Bangkok. "Steep, too. Don't suppose you're coming to help?"

"I'm strictly admin, Ewan, you know that. Logistics, planning." Fraser waved a half-filled pint glass of red wine, as if that somehow explained his considerable managerial duties.

"You're strictly something all right." Bangkok grumbled as he closed the van's doors, and the pair of them made their way around the building towards the stepped path at the back of the hotel.

"Anyway, Jake here will give you a hand." Duncan turned and called back. "Clean the brushes, or whatever you have to do, then follow Ewan up, all right?" He didn't wait for an answer, and Jake watched them disappear around the corner.

This was bad. Maybe only a bit bad, but potentially very bad. And conceivably, disastrously bad.

What would drone footage of the bay show? Nothing, if everyone was hidden away and not, for example, engaged in hand-to-hand fairy-gremlin combat training on the beach. That would be the money shot to end all money shots, as far as Duncan was concerned.

But assume the Trogirans were out of sight and under cover, as agreed. Was there anything else that could give them away?

Jake wasn't sure, but '4k, 360-degree mode' sounded like a lot of surveillance power. Strang's boathouse was open to the water on the offshore side. If Bangkok got the drone down close enough, would the elevator chute be visible? The antenna dish in the eaves? Someone might wonder what those were?

Or, from on high on a sunny, blue-sky day – would you be able to see the line of the chute stretching from under the boathouse and descending into the loch and out into the sound?

Or, shit, what if, from two hundred feet above the still, clear water you could see something on the bottom? Even that far down? Something large enough to make viewers look twice? A shadow, a shape, an outline, that made you go, "Wait a minute, is that a – it can't be – Jesus, call the police, or – I don't know – the army or something."

Bad, very bad, disastrously bad. Those were the choices, and Jake couldn't take the chance.

He had at least to warn Ruan, and Alva, who was up at the house today. Which would mean ignoring Duncan – not the worst thing in the world – but also borrowing Jimmy's Land Rover without permission.

Bollocks.

Jake was on his way around the other side of the building, just as Dougie staggered out.

"Sorry Dougie, emergency," he said, as he passed. "I'll sort the paint brushes out later."

There was a growl, and what sounded like "Rip ma

knittin," but Jake didn't linger. The Land Rover was parked where it always was, outside the hotel kitchen door at the rear, and Jake jumped in.

He sat in silence for a second. No angry shout from a shaven-headed punk crooner licensee. That was something. He'd deal with the fallout later.

The keys were where they always were. In the ignition. As Jimmy had said, when Jake had once expressed surprise, "Anyone takes the Landy without permission, I would be gravely disappointed and would unleash my dogs of war." Which was clear enough, though Jake had to give points to Jimmy for knowing his *Mad Max*.

He started the engine, with trepidation, backed the vehicle out, and rolled onto the quayside and down the road out of the village. Checked the rear-view mirror. No irate landlord, no dogs of war.

Jake knew from experience that it would take Ewan fifteen, twenty minutes to climb up the steps and path, and head across the heather to the brow of the hill. Almost certainly longer, lugging his drone kit, which he then had to unpack, set up and launch. Say forty minutes until he had his bird in the air.

That was plenty of time to drive the three miles or so around to Strang's place, and tell them what was happening. He doubted there was anything they could do about it, but forewarned was forearmed. They could at least go down to the beach and check it all looked, well – normal. Free of aliens. That sort of thing. Perhaps even summon the General on the old fairy-phone and tell him to employ the Trogiran cloaking device. They must have one of those, surely?

He took the turn from the road at speed, tyres screeching, and sped on into the woods. The fence and gate were coming up fast, and Jake had been holding out hope that it was open, given that Alva had driven up earlier that day. He saw that the gate was closed across the road. Slowed, stopped, and got out.

Come on, Alva. Just for once, you didn't lock it behind you.

Bugger. You did.

He rattled the chain and lock. If he left the Land Rover here, jumped the gate and ran up the track to the house, that would easily take another ten minutes. Too long. So, that just left…

Bollocks.

Jake hopped back into the driver's seat, and carefully reversed down the lane and stopped a hundred yards from the gate. Selected first gear, looked straight ahead in the direction of travel, hands on the steering wheel at ten to two.

That was all textbook. It was the next bit that they didn't cover in the Highway Code and driving test.

He put his foot down, picking up speed, shuffling through the gears. Kept his hands and arms rigid, eyes on the rapidly approaching gate, and only flinched at the last second as the Land Rover ploughed through, wood splintering on either side. Part of the snapped chain flew up and cracked against the windscreen, leaving a visible chip on the glass. Jake swerved slightly with the impact, but wrestled the vehicle back in line, and roared on up the lane. He could see the shattered remains of the gate strewn across the road behind him, and the tell-tale glints of broken headlight shards.

In anyone's book, that was a pranging. Jimmy was going to be furious. There would be ructions, with many, many Rs. Jake had no idea how he was going to explain any of it. But right now, none of that mattered.

He reached the house in a couple of heart-pounding minutes and slammed the brakes on, blaring the horn as he did so.

That brought Alva out, scowl firmly in place.

"What is it about *not* drawing attention to ourselves that you don't get? And why are you in Jimmy's Land Rover? And what the hell have you *done* to Jimmy's Land Rover? Is that a bit of the gate? What have you done to the gate?"

All good questions. No time to answer them.

Ruan had followed, and behind him hovered the General at shoulder height. Jake could hear him chuntering, "What the dickens is this racket?"

"He can't be out here," said Jake, pointing at the General. "None of them can."

He moved forward, and tried to whoosh the General back inside, putting his hands for the first time on the creature, steering him towards the door. No time to appreciate what a momentous occasion that was — literally, first contact with an alien being. He could feel a gentle thrum as his hands settled on the General's tunic and body, felt the wispy breeze of his wings as the airborne Trogiran pushed back.

"Take your hands off me, sir! This is most inappropriate. I've had chaps court-martialled for less."

"What *is* going on?" Arms folded, dagger eyes, vintage Alva.

"We've got a problem," said Jake. "Indoors, now."

Chapter 31

It was worse than Jake had feared. It wasn't just the General out on a little holiday. There were at least half a dozen Trogirans inside the house, making themselves comfortable.

"What are they all doing here?" Apart from watching *Downton Abbey*, it seemed. He looked over at the dining table, where the crumbed remains of chicken nuggets were scattered. "Oh, right."

"I know," said Alva. "Ruan brought them up. He felt sorry for them." She shook her head in despair.

"Ach, Alva, look at their wee faces. If they can't do their exercises, they have to have something to look forward to. Can't stay cooped up in their wee spaceship all the time."

"They can," said Jake. "They have to, that's the whole point. You have no idea how dangerous it is for them to be outside today." He told them about Duncan's plan for the drone footage. "Bangkok's up there now," he said. "On the cliff, getting the thing ready. Might be up in the air by now for all I know. This was the worst possible day to choose for a TV meal-deal outing. They shouldn't be away from the ship at all."

"What's all this?" said the General, still bristling at being handled. "Danger, you say? Another agent? Infernal fellows. Reproducing at will now, are they?"

"Not an agent," said Jake. "A drone."

"Killer drone? Laser cannon, I assume? Yes, I recall the trouble we had repelling those in the first Niksic advance. I can see we've underestimated this Agent Armstrong. Lieutenant!" The General barked at one of the creatures on the sofa. "Prepare to return to the vessel, we need to ready the anti-drone blasters."

There was a ripple of excited movement along the sofa, with the Trogirans clearly torn between staying to watch Maggie Smith tear a strip off an unfortunate chambermaid and unleashing heavy weaponry upon a middle-aged estate agent.

God almighty. They were behaving like primary-school kids hopped up on Haribos who'd just found the keys to the NERF gun cupboard.

"No one is going anywhere," said Jake. "It's imperative that you all stay inside."

Imperative? The General's speech patterns were beginning to rub off on him now. Still, if it made them all shut up and listen.

"Ewan Robertson," growled Strang. "He's always

been a wee bastard. Him and his electric banjo. If I catch him on my land – "

"That's not helping either. Look, if we stay inside for now, we'll be fine. Then we need to talk seriously about what staying hidden means. I'm assuming there's nothing else for the drone to see? You haven't got anyone on manoeuvres down on the beach? And I've been wondering whether a drone might be able to pick out the shape of the ship under the water? Do you think that's possible?"

"Worry not," said the General. "The vessel lies at a depth of one thousand feet and is fully cloaked."

Jake allowed himself a half smile. Knew it. Ask him anything about alien spaceship technology. For the first time in half an hour he began to relax. This would probably be all right.

"The issue as I see it," said the General, "concerns the chaps who are due to relieve us shortly. They will be exposed under the enemy drone, and while their training is such that – "

"What?" said Jake and Alva.

"The usual rota," said the General. "I left orders. No one ever wants to miss a feast supplied by Lord Strang." He bowed his head in recognition. "Most kind, as always."

"Oh, god," said Alva.

"They'll all be coming up, see, in groups?" said Ruan. "They love their wee feast, you know they do." At which point, the consequences of that seemed to dawn on him. "Alva, I'm sorry. I didn't think."

"What are the chances," said Jake, "of your chaps not coming? Busy, maybe, on the ship?"

"Disobeying an order?" said the General, as if the concept had never occurred to him before. "Does anyone disobey the Dowager Countess Crawley, I think not! No, the chaps will be here, as required."

"Then someone's going to have to stop them," said Alva.

"Right, yes, of course Lady Alva, understood." The General fluttered over to the door.

"Not you!" Jake and Alva were finding themselves combining nicely by now. Jake moved to the door, wondering how you would tackle a flying gremlin. He didn't want to have to sit on the General, but it might come to that.

"I'll go," said Alva to Jake. "You don't know how to operate the elevator intercom. It'll be fine, I'll tell them to stay put. And if the drone films me, there's nothing unusual about me being here, having a walk on the beach."

It sounded like she was convincing herself, but Jake had to agree it was the best option they had.

"Understood?" she said pointedly to the General. "You're to stay here, with your crew, until I come back and tell you it's safe to leave."

"Absolutely, Lady Alva. Discretion the better part of valour. Though I still think we could blast the miscreant out of the sky, if only you'd allow – "

"No!" said the Alva-Jake double-act.

"Quite," said the General. "Your planet, your show, entirely understand. Carry on."

"It's all my fault, Alva, let me go instead." Ruan appeared distraught, wringing his hands. "I should have sent the little nuggets down the chute instead. What was I thinking? I'll never forgive myself if that bastard films the wee fellas. They'll be on the television and everything. They'll take them away, and then what will we do?" He seemed inconsolable.

"Ruan, it's fine." Alva shook his shoulder, looked him in the eye. "I'll be quicker. You stay here. There's nothing to worry about, I promise."

This time, she didn't sound as convinced, but Ruan didn't notice.

"Young Robertson, always a wee bastard," he said again. "Sneaky, like his father. Up on the cliff, is he? Spying on my land! I'll do for him!"

"You're going to stay here, all right? Keep the General and his crew entertained, isn't that right, General? I'll be back as quickly as I can."

Alva led Ruan to the sofa and sat him between the crew. She went to the sideboard and poured him a large whisky, said a few words to the General who nodded, and then turned for the door. Jake was waiting for her.

"It'll be fine," he said.

"I think so. If they're not in the boathouse yet — haven't left the ship — I can stop any of them coming up. If they're out already, they just have the beach to cross, before they reach cover in the glen. We'd have to be pretty unlucky for Bangkok to have his drone right overhead for that short period. And anyway, look." She showed Jake a folded blanket. "If they're out and I hear or see the drone, I'll throw this over them."

"Good thinking."

"I thought so." She gave Jake a rare smile. "It's going to be all right." This time, she sounded more positive, but by now she probably couldn't bear to think otherwise.

"Good luck." Without thinking, Jake reached for a hand, and there was an awkward clasp as she used the other to open the door.

First time touching an alien, first time touching Alva. This was turning out to be quite a day.

"Hand?" she said, smiling again. "I'll need that."

"Right, sorry, yes."

And then she was gone, sprinting down the path and out through the gate into the glen.

Jake watched her go until she disappeared into the trees. He closed the door behind him and walked across the room to pull the curtains. Perhaps a bit excessive, but right now he was thinking of nothing but prying eyes and hovering drones.

The General and his crew were perched in a line along the back of the sofa. Maggie Smith was pursing her lips. A chambermaid was crying. The Trogirans were chortling away. The whisky bottle on the coffee table was a good inch lower than it had been.

Maybe this would be all right, after all? With any luck, this wasn't the day that earthlings discovered that they weren't alone in the universe.

Just one thing, though. There was the whisky bottle. There was the empty tumbler. "Where's Ruan?" said Jake.

"Ah, yes," said the General. "Lord Strang had to slip out on confidential business." He pointed through the lounge door, down the corridor towards the kitchen, where Jake could see the open side door that led outside.

"What business?"

"He didn't say. Although of course a nobleman's business is his own. I didn't pry. He'll be back shortly, I'm sure."

Jake was less certain about that. He'd just spotted the empty hooks on the wall by the door.

The silly old fool.

The side door was open, and Ruan was gone. And so was his shotgun.

Chapter 32

Jake vaulted the gate at the end of the path and sprinted into the trees. The main track ran down the glen towards the loch, under cover of towering trunks and branches.

No sign of Ruan ahead, but he'd had a fair start, and there were several other side trails that he could have taken which wound through the trees to various points along the beach.

To the pier and boathouse first. Check with Alva that the next Trogiran landing party had been fore-warned. That was the priority.

He burst onto the beach and stopped, casting his eyes in an arc and listening for the tell-tale buzz of a drone. Nothing. And still no sign of Ruan. Perhaps he'd gone to the boathouse, too, in a misguided show of support?

Jake ran across the sands. He could see the pier-side

boathouse door was open and, as he pounded the boardwalk and got closer, there was Alva, standing over the video screen by the elevator chute.

She turned at the sound of his feet.

"I thought you were staying at the house?"

"It's Ruan. He's gone. Slipped away. Missing. He's not here?"

There was a muffled exclamation from the screen, where a heavily whiskered Trogiran was looking quizzical.

"Everything all right, m'lady?"

Alva looked flustered. "Yes, thank you, lieutenant. As I said, you're all to remain in your quarters, as per the General's revised orders."

"And the Lord Strang? Missing?"

"He can't have gone far, don't worry. I'm sure he's out – patrolling the borders?"

Alva pulled a face at Jake and gave a who-knows shrug. He moved to the boathouse door, peered out and scanned the beach. Nothing.

"Understood, m'lady. Standing by." The screen crackled and the video feed cut out.

"Well, where the hell is he?" said Alva. 'He had one job. Which was to watch *Downton Abbey* with his wee pals."

"No idea," said Jake. "And don't get mad, but he's got his shotgun with him."

"Christ. That's all we need. I've just spent five minutes persuading this lot not to arm the laser-blasters."

"You don't think he'd do anything stupid, do you?"

"He's a man. Of course I do." Alva's eyes flashed.

"Harsh."

"Have you met the men in my life?"

Duncan, Jimmy, Strang, and arguably the General and all his little gung-ho space warriors. Fair enough, she had a point, though Jake was a little discouraged to be included in the roster, so he changed the subject.

"What about Bangkok and his drone? I didn't see any sign of it."

"Me neither. That's something I suppose. Right, let's go find Calamity Strang, before anything else kicks off."

The video screen crackled again, and the lieutenant reappeared.

"M'lady, the chaps in the vessel's surveillance unit are reporting activity on the southern border."

Alva and Jake exchanged a look. The cliffs above the loch, in the direction of the village.

"The drone? You've detected the drone?"

"Negative, m'lady. It's not an aerial incursion. Ground-based bipedal humanoid, is my chaps' best guess."

That had to be Bangkok. He'd finally lugged his gear to the top. Well, let him do his worst. Nothing to see here, except the natural beauty of the isle of Elsay, shimmering in the haze of a beautiful summer's day.

"They are also now reporting a second ground-based incursion."

"What?"

The Alva-Jake query combo was back in business.

"Approaching from the northwest. Breaking cover from the forest, ascending on a lateral interception course. Bipedal humanoid."

Up and across the hillside from the glen behind the beach.

Ruan Strang.

Bollocks.

"Thank you, lieutenant, we'll take it from here. Let's go." Alva tapped a symbol on the screen, the video winked out, and they dashed from the boathouse, pausing only to lock the door behind them.

Standing on the beach, for the first time they could hear the high-pitched buzz of a drone. It was difficult to pick out at this distance – the speck could have been a bird – but as they followed the noise and adjusted their eyes, there it was. High in the sky, coming from the direction of the cliffs, heading for its first pass over the loch.

"There!" said Jake, pointing.

Another speck, on the clifftop. Impossible to identify at this distance, but clearly a person, in line of sight of the drone.

"That's Bangkok. So, where's Ruan?"

"Dunno, come on." Jake led the way, running across the beach. "This is the quickest way up, over those rocks at the end. We'll head him off, and with any luck Bangkok never even needs to know there's a homicidal old sod after him."

They made it across the beach in under a minute, sticking to the firmer sand by the shoreline. Jake scrambled up the tumbled rocks under the cliff – the ones he'd fallen off, what seemed like a lifetime ago. Stretched out a hand for Alva, who grabbed it to steady herself as she made the first climb.

"There's a rough path starts just here," said Jake, pulling her up again. "Zigzags up to the top."

Alva looked doubtful.

"Trust me."

On the grassy bluff underneath the overhanging gorse bushes, they could no longer see the clifftop, or Bangkok, but they could still hear the drone as it swept the loch.

They hiked up the path, clearing the gorse, and were soon on the open cliffside, looking either up the steep slope ahead or down across the water. It was hardly a path, more of a sheep track, cutting through the heather and switching direction at times – foothold to foothold, open patch to open patch.

Other tracks came in from the right, following a similarly lazy meander up from the trees at the back of the beach. A flash of movement above caught their eye, and there – suddenly – was Ruan, perhaps thirty feet higher than them, heading on a flatter trajectory for the summit.

"Ruan! Ruan!"

The old man didn't hear Alva, or ignored her. But they could hear him, in the still summer air.

"You wee bastard! Get off my land!"

They climbed faster, cutting straight up the hillside, wading through the stands of heather. Ruan came in and out of view as they got closer, but he was ahead of them now, zeroing in on Bangkok and the summit.

"They're my wee pals, not yours! I'll show you what's what!"

Ruan cast a shadow on the hillside as he went – the silhouette of a determined, marching man with a shotgun slung over his shoulder.

"God," said Alva. "Should never have given him the whisky. I thought it might calm him down." She panted with the effort and took a beat, doubled over, then scrambled upwards again, Jake in her wake.

They were almost on Ruan's path now, which lay a few steps above, but he was a good thirty feet beyond them. They gained the path and followed, Ruan bobbing in front of them as he loped forward, shouting.

"Where are you, Robertson, ya wee bastard!"

They heard an indistinct, answering shout and, rounding a curve, saw that it was Bangkok, drone console in both hands, on the highest point of the cliff. He was facing out across the loch, with Ruan approaching rapidly from his lefthand side, shotgun now cradled over one arm.

Bangkok turned to see him, looked down for a quick check of the monitor on his console, and then looked back at Ruan. Maybe now twenty feet away, Jake and Alva twenty feet behind him.

"Aye aye! Here he is, the Fairy King! Wondered if you'd be about."

Ruan stopped and delved into a side pocket, and Jake and Alva paused, too, unwilling to spook the old man if they could help it. Like Bangkok, they were close enough to hear the soft 'chunk' as Strang closed the gun, and the metallic click as he slid the safety catch forward.

"What are you doing, you mad old – "

Ruan pointed the shotgun high in the sky and pulled the trigger. The blast echoed across the hillside.

"You're not taking away my wee pals!"

"Fuckin' hell, man." Bangkok ducked instinctively and lost his grip on the console, which dropped to the ground. He scrambled after it, cursing. Picked it back up and desperately tried to regain control of the unseen drone, though as he now also had one extremely wary eye on a trigger-happy drunk, it didn't seem to be going too well.

"I mean it," roared Ruan. "Off my land!"

"Ruan, man, seriously. Let me get the wee drone in, I'll be gone. You mad old sod." Bangkok muttered the last phrase, risked another look at the console and then feverishly scanned the sky. "Ach, no, I'm gonna lose it." He paddled the joysticks, a furious look on his face. "Ya bastard thing!"

Ruan aimed the shotgun, this time drawing down directly on Bangkok. "I'm warning you! Last chance!"

"Fuck off, Ruan, will you, this thing cost a thousand pounds. I'm not dropping it in the ocean because you don't like – oh, shit, no, come on, you've got to be kidding." Bangkok wailed the last few words.

"We have to do something!" Jake pawed at Alva's elbow, pointing at the debacle unfolding before them.

"Well, thank you very much." Bangkok shouted through gritted teeth as he threw the console to the ground. "It's gone, you happy now? You mad old git. I wasn't doing any harm."

"Spying! On the wee fellas! I told you all what would happen if you came here, on my land."

"Away with you, man. You and your fairies. You're soft in the head. You should be locked up."

"My wee pals, they're worth ten of you! Don't you worry, General, I'll see the bastard off." Strang was waving the shotgun around erratically now, but Bangkok was so livid about the loss of his drone that he took a step or two forwards. Ruan roared at him again.

Bangkok took another step and then noticed Jake and Alva for the first time, inching slowly closer.

"You come for him? Good, about time. He wants locking up, Alva, pet. Bloody danger, he is. And I'm billing you for my drone, you hear me?" Bangkok shouted at Ruan.

The old man jerked his head and shoulders round, saw Alva and Jake behind him. The shotgun followed him, so now it was pointing at them.

"Whoa, Ruan, easy, all right?" said Alva. "Let's not do anything rash. It's all going to be fine." She looked from Ruan to Jake and back again, smiling reassuringly, making calming gestures. Jake didn't know about Alva, but he was less sure it would all be fine, having had Ruan fire a shotgun at him once before. He hadn't hesitated on that occasion – had discharged the gun straight at the Land Rover – and didn't look as if he would now.

Ruan adjusted his feet, shook his head, as if clearing his sight.

"Fine? Like bollocks it is," yelled Bangkok. "Cost me a drone, he has."

Ruan's head whipped round again, facing Bangkok, and this time he stumbled. The gun barrel jerked upwards as Ruan fell backwards, catching his foot in dense heather. The report was just as loud as before, the gun discharging harmlessly into the sky. Bangkok had ducked again in any case, so didn't see what happened.

But Jake did.

Almost in slow motion. As people often say happens, in incidents or accidents. As if time slows, so you experience every detail. See it frame by frame.

Ruan bent and crumpled as he fell, one hand still clinging to the shotgun. He tumbled and rolled once, twice, and then bounced – that was exactly the word – off springy turf that catapulted him off the edge of the cliff.

There was a strangled cry, and then nothing.

Seconds of pure silence in the calm summer air, save for a guttural moan from Alva.

And eventually a faint noise that Jake would

remember for the rest of his life, but hoped he had imagined.

A dull, wet thud – as if a large object comprised of sixty percent water had fallen a hundred feet onto the rocks below.

Chapter 33

They had waited until well after sunset to go down to the beach, walking in silence through the dense, dark trees of the glen.

A bright moon in a clear sky threw a sparkling shaft of light across the loch. The cliffs on the far side of the beach were swathed in shadows, with only the ridge line of the summit visible against the pale, late-night sky.

"Ready?" said Jake.

Alva nodded. "Ready."

She didn't look ready, but the General had been adamant, regardless of any danger of discovery. A salute to their fallen comrade, Lord Strang. It was their way, and the chaps would expect it. Lady Alva and Jake's presence was required. The ceremony would commence at midnight.

It had been three days since Ruan's fatal fall, and the consequences were still unfurling.

The three of them – Jake, Alva and Bangkok Ewan – had reacted in horror, frozen at first, unable to believe what had happened. They had peered gingerly over the edge, and while they didn't see a body, none of them was in any doubt. Ruan couldn't have survived the fall.

They had raced back to the village to raise the alarm, across the heather and down the rough track and steps to the rear of the hotel.

At first, it had been hard to get anyone to understand. Ruan Strang? On the cliffs? A drone? Gun? What do you mean, fell?

Duncan had grasped it the quickest and made the necessary calls, and Jimmy had commandeered the lads from his band and put a boat out from the harbour. Jake watched it go, a dark shape in the distance with a single light on deck that disappeared as it rounded the pier and breakwater.

The boat had returned an hour later, the men sombre and wet to the waist. A rumpled tarpaulin was laid out on deck. When Duncan went to lift a corner, Jimmy had shaken his head. "No," he had said, "best not."

They had fetched a stretcher and Jimmy, showing a previously unseen tenderness, spoke softly as he directed the careful transfer of the covered body. "All right, Ruan," he'd said, and gently touched the canvas – a three-fingered benediction on a raised mound at one end. Ruan had been laid in an unused parlour room at the hotel, from which Jimmy – island landlord, taxi driver and emergency undertaker – had emerged some while later, with scrubbed hands and arms, and an unreadable face.

"Come on, let's go."

Jake, for once, led Alva to the boathouse and unlocked the door. Moonlight illuminated the interior from the side open to the water. Alva tapped the chute to make the screen appear, ran the usual call sequence, and stepped back. The machine hummed and the lights began to flash.

She'd been quiet for days, which was unusual. Shock, perhaps? Jake could understand that – he could still see Ruan's fall and hear the thud on the rocks every time he closed his eyes and tried to sleep.

But there was fear and worry, too, that everything had now changed irrevocably. That Ruan's death was going to unleash a chain of events that resulted – sooner or later – in his, their, great secret being revealed. For this reason, she had been dead against the ceremony from the outset, but the General wasn't for turning.

In the meantime, the police had sent someone from the mainland and taken statements. A recluse with a history of erratic behaviour and drunken threats. Yes, he had a licence for the gun. No, no one had thought he was dangerous. A bit cracked, confused, maybe, but that was as far as it went.

All that stuff about fairies, that he'd been shouting on the clifftop? All in his head. In the end, simply a tragic accident. Could have been worse, at least he didn't shoot Bangkok (or 'Bang-Bangkok' as one of the more mordant bar regulars had since dubbed him).

Jake and Alva hadn't even had to lie. Just told the story straight. They had been doing their best to look out for an elderly, lonely, widowed islander. Only wished they had noticed earlier that he'd slipped out of the house. Yes, he'd been agitated about the drone flyover of the bay. Mr Strang was very protective of his land. They'd seen him on the cliffs and had tried to get there in time, to stop him hurting himself or anyone else. He'd tripped and fallen; they'd seen it all.

Strang's body had gone back on the midweek ferry with the police. The death had to be reported to the coroner, but a post-mortem or inquest was unlikely. Ultimately, it was agreed, everyone had done everything they could.

Nothing more to look into, that would be all. Case closed.

In the boathouse, the lights on the screen stopped flashing and, after a short pause and some intermittent rumbling sounds, the first Trogiran popped out of the chute in a flurry of wings and whiskers. They fluttered briefly in the air and dropped to the decked boathouse floor. Same dark blue uniform that they always wore, but this time with the addition of a purple sash across the body and a small, black tricorn hat. Like a little Napoleon, popping up from the depths.

The creature snapped a smart salute at Alva and

Jake and shuffled along the floor, away from the chute. One after another followed, all dressed similarly, saluting each time as they hit the ground, forming two guard lines.

Still they kept coming, and Jake was taken aback. This wasn't the usual half a dozen, or even the twenty or so that he seen rehearsing combat manoeuvres on the beach. He counted thirty, forty, and finally forty-eight, assembled in two rows. This was, it seemed, the entire ship's company.

Last out was the General, who hovered at shoulder height and laid a clawed hand on Alva's forearm, nodding solemnly before dropping to the deck.

"Company advance," he ordered from the rear. "Air transit, ceremonial formation."

The two lines of Trogirans turned as one to the open door, rose in the air together, leaned forward and flew straight out of the boathouse. The water below the deck rippled in the draught as the last two exited, with the General following behind at a stately pace.

Jake and Alva emerged onto the pier and jumped down to the beach. Fifty yards away, the company had reassembled on the ground, this time in a half-circle, with the two ends at the water's edge and the General in the middle, facing inwards. He launched himself a few feet in the air, over the company's heads, and beckoned Jake and Alva over, dropping to the sand again when they had entered the circle.

There was still a faint hint of warmth in the air, but

it was otherwise dark, quiet and still. The slight lap of the water, a hoot of an owl from somewhere in the glen, and the gleam of polished buttons on the tunics of an alien honour guard.

"Your loss is our loss," said the General. "Lord Strang was our First Protector and a great friend to the Trogiran people."

There was a rippled thump as forty-eight small right arms slapped across forty-eight small chests.

"He opened his home to strangers. This great land of his" – the General swept his arms wide, as though the whole planet was Ruan Strang's – "afforded us shelter and safety."

Another rippled thump.

"He died as he lived, protecting his friends. We shall never forget him, and will always honour him, for as long as we endure."

Another thump.

This was making Ruan Strang out to be a cross between Optimus Prime and Nelson Mandela. Ruan, whose trousers had been kept up by a length of string. No matter, Jake had a lump in his throat, and he daren't look at Alva, though he could hear her sniffling.

"Lady Alva, if you please?"

She took a photograph from her jacket, leaned down and handed it to the General. He held it in his clawed hands, bowed his head, and then snapped back to attention.

"Gentlemen, present arms!"

Jake shot a worried glanced at Alva. He'd seen first-hand what those things could do. The General surely wasn't going to launch a forty-eight thermo-wand salute? Hidden in a dark inlet at midnight, as they were, he must know they still had to keep the ceremony explosion-free?

The batons were drawn but not extended, and each Trogiran held theirs in front of them, like they were holding a tiny flagpole, pointing out at forty-five degrees.

"Engage wands."

For once, Jake didn't inwardly snigger at the word. A white light on each wand tip was illuminated at the General's command. He rose once more, wings flut-tering slightly, and hovered in front of Jake and Alva, holding the photograph out flat and face-up in front of him.

Ruan and Eileen Strang on their wedding day, young and beautiful, beaming at the camera.

"Touch the image, if you please, Lady Alva and Jake."

They each placed a finger on the photograph and, instinctively, reached down to grasp each other's free hand. It was a nice moment, standing there in the night air, looking past the General, still hovering. Gazing out over the water. Holding hands. Honouring Ruan Strang.

Jake had never been to a funeral or memorial service before, but he didn't see how this one would ever be beaten. Cucumber sandwiches in the back room of a pub just weren't going to cut it.

Alva squeezed his hand – hello, interesting? – and, encouraged, he squeezed back.

"No, you dolt, look!" She gave an exaggerated nod towards the water.

It started as a shimmer, perhaps ten yards out in the shallows – a flicker in the loch that became a spreading, swirling pool of light. It spun and rose in a silver-tinged cylinder, which pulsed and bulged before shaping itself into a life-sized human figure – Ruan Strang in his wedding suit.

As he turned slowly and gracefully, feet barely touching the water, he aged before their eyes, until he was the Ruan they knew. The Ruan in worn corduroys and a battered cap, with a lined face and an unkempt beard. The Ruan who had died trying to save his friends.

A second pool of light began to swirl, and there was young Eileen, in her elegant, white wedding dress and a twinkly smile that would last almost another forty years. Before their eyes, she aged, too, eventually a match for the other photograph on Ruan's mantelpiece – the one taken a year before she'd died. The Eileen whose death had broken Ruan.

The two figures reached for each other's hand and turned for the open water. Were they running or dancing? Jake couldn't tell, he could only see them bob and weave as they tacked slowly across the loch, flitting over the water.

And then they simply rose and rose and rose —
disappearing shadows in the night sky — before winking
out with a final, piercing burst of light.

"Back to the stars," said the General. "As, one day,
we all shall travel. Farewell, my friend."

Chapter 34

"Bad business, Jake."

Bad for *his* business, Duncan probably meant, but Jake gave him the benefit of the doubt.

The whole village had been in sombre mood for a couple of weeks now. Ruan Strang might have been more tolerated than loved, but no one had wanted him to plummet to his death from a cliff. Except possibly Bangkok Ewan, who was still smarting over the loss of his drone.

Things continued as normal – Mrs Dunmore opened the general store when she felt like it, a few cyclists came and went on the ferry, Fraser Souvenirs sold a handful of Peruvian snow globes – but no one's heart seemed in it.

Duncan himself was itching to get on with the sale of the hotel, and only decorum was stopping him. Well, decorum and the fear of what Alva might say if he ignored the mood of the village, and her strongly expressed views, and cracked on with making himself 800,000 pounds richer.

Consequently, Jake had been taken off hotel-painting duties and stationed in the gift shop a couple of times a week, with Alva nowhere to be seen.

That was also apparently a 'bad business,' with Duncan just pursing his lips and shuddering when asked if she was all right.

"A bit upset, lad," was all he'd say. "She's taken it harder than you'd think. I know she looked out for him, but I didn't realise they were that close. I don't know, maybe there's more to it?"

Jake had been non-committal. Duncan had *no* idea.

"Anyway," said Duncan, locking the door to the shop. "Not a bad day. Might go down the snow globe route, what do you reckon?"

"Interesting," said Jake, having learned the hard way that having a definite opinion on something like this meant taking delivery the next week of a thousand mixed South American snow globes, and then being blamed when they didn't sell.

"Good lad. See you at Saturday drinks?"

There was the usual crowd in the hotel bar, and Jake took a seat in Duncan's booth and sipped his Little Widdle. Honestly, if you closed your eyes and imagined you were drinking a nice, cold lager and not lukewarm bath water, it wasn't *that* bad.

Jake was grateful to be drinking anything at all in the bar of the Port Hotel, given that he'd pranged the landlord's Land Rover on the day of Ruan's death and couldn't even begin to explain why. Jimmy, it was safe to say, had been displeased at the whole Land Rover-meets-gate incident – never mind that Jake had taken the vehicle in the first place without asking.

He had only got away with it after Alva's intervention, agreed between the pair of them – that she had called Jake in a panic, realising that Ruan had gone AWOL, and he had rushed up there in the Land Rover at her insistence, busting through the gate in his haste. They drew a veil over the obvious flaws in this flimsy explanation – primarily that Jake didn't even have a phone any longer – hoping that the shock of Ruan Strang's death would distract Jimmy from making further enquiries.

It had worked. Not even Jimmy of the fearsome bulk and Vulcan death grip had wanted to cross-examine Alva in her current low mood. The pranged Land Rover went unquestioned, and the village as a whole remained uncertain as to how to behave. Conversations in the bar were hushed – as if no one wanted to be the first to raise their voice. Even Jimmy's familiar growl had been dialled back to a low rasp.

It was no different tonight, even though there was already a crowd in. Some desultory chat, and the occasional scrape of a chair as people went to the bar.

Bangkok was over in the corner with the other members of the band, and one of them picked up a fiddle in a quiet moment and laid down a gentle air. Something soft and melancholy that rose and fell like a boat on the tide.

Another fiddle joined in, at which Bangkok reached for his guitar and picked out a quiet melody that filled the boat's sails. Underneath, the second guitarist blew a breeze across its bows, and all four musicians then took the tune and carried it to its conclusion, dropping away one by one until the last remaining fiddle drew out a final, poignant note.

There was a silence in the room, broken by Jimmy at the bar, raising a glass.

"To Ruan," he said.

The room repeated his name.

"The Fairy King," said Bangkok, from his stool in the corner, raising his own glass.

There was a slight intake of breath from somewhere in the room, but Bangkok kept his glass held high and his countenance sincere.

"Aye, the Fairy King," said Jimmy. "Rest in peace. Now then, who's for a wee dram on the house?"

That ended predictably – Bangkok crowd-surfing from the bar, Jimmy belting out 'Livin' on a Prayer' – but it lifted the pall that had covered Port Levin since Ruan's death.

That just left Alva to deal with, and Duncan had a plan for that. His usual cunning plan in circumstances such as this.

"Come up to the house tomorrow night for a family dinner?"

"Are you sure? Isn't she – ? "

"Ah, she'll be fine with it. Do her good."

"If you say so."

"I do. We're having a lamb roast. Tell you what goes nicely with that?"

"Let me guess."

Which is why Jake found himself back on the Fraser doorstep clutching a bottle of Rioja, with Alva saying, "What are you doing here? Oh, right, of course he did. You better come in."

Duncan babbled away during dinner, trying on occasion to steer the conversation towards the benefit of getting on with things, not looking back but forwards, thinking of the future, and grasping opportunities when they presented themselves. "Oh, not about selling the hotel, goodness me, no Alva, just, you know…"

And when that went nowhere, Duncan cleared the dishes away from the table, gave Jake a huge stage wink, and disappeared off into the lounge to watch TV.

At least he didn't use the word 'lovebirds' at any point.

Jake sat there for a while, uncertain where to start.

"If you're here to cheer me up," said Alva, "let's at least sit outside. He's driving me mad."

She led him through the lounge and out through the French doors into the garden, glaring at Duncan as she left. He didn't notice, being fully occupied with slapping the TV and questioning its parentage – there was a white, snowy fuzz across the screen that endured whichever channel he chose.

Jake sat next to her on the bench, and they gazed

out over the water as the light slowly faded from the sky.

"How are you? Really?" he said.

There was a pause. "I feel so tired." Alva slumped a little, her shoulder resting against his. "I know what everyone thought about him, but I shared something with Ruan. Something extraordinary. And now he's gone, there's only me to deal with it all. With them, and with what's coming. What's going to happen to Ruan's house? What reason do I have now to keep going up there? It's exhausting."

"It's not just you," said Jake. "You don't have to do it on your own. There's me, too."

"You're not going to stick around though, are you? You can't. Holidays come to an end at some point. You don't even have a proper job here. You'll go back to college eventually."

"I don't know about that," said Jake, which came as a surprise to him. Was *that* what he was thinking? That he might stay? How would that work? It would be August in a week or so, but term didn't start again for almost another couple of months. That was a long time to last without a job.

"Don't be daft, of course you will. What have you got to stay for?"

"Apart from the aliens in the loch, you mean?"

She allowed herself the faintest of smiles at that, and settled further into his shoulder.

Duncan appeared on the terrace at the top of the garden and shouted something about his TV reception.

Alva stirred herself, turned and gave him a not-now-Duncan broadside, and resumed her position – arm against arm on the bench, head leaned towards Jake's shoulder.

Hmm.

Was this the answer to the question, "What have you got to stay for?"

Wisely perhaps – or maybe not – Jake said nothing, not wanting to spoil the moment. You never knew which way things would go with Alva, and this was hands down the most intimate contact he had had with her since his arrival.

"I just don't want it to end," she said.

Jake didn't misunderstand this. She meant the ship in the loch, the Trogirans, the secret aliens. Although part of him wondered how far that 'it' might extend, if he did decide to stay?

"Me neither," he said. "They're pretty cool, for half-pint aliens."

But it might end, at any point. However closely they guarded their secret, it would only take one slip.

He thought back to the vision of Ruan and Eileen dancing across the water, and wondered again why Alva had never asked the General to let her see her long-dead mother? It bothered him, though he couldn't say why. Perhaps because time might be running out?

"Can I ask you something?"

Alva didn't move, but shifted her head slightly on his shoulder, which Jake took as a nod.

"That was an extraordinary thing they did, out on

the loch that night. Wouldn't you want to see your mum like that? Just once?"

He heard a deep sigh and hoped he hadn't ruined the mood. But Alva kept her head where it was – didn't rear up, eyes blazing.

"You don't think I've thought about it?" she said, in a low voice. "But I made my peace with things a long time ago. Mum died when I was eight. I remember her, of course I do, but only fragments. I missed out on everything else, growing up without a mum. Nothing against Duncan, he did his best."

She paused, and Jake said nothing. Thinking there was probably more, but also not knowing what to say.

"They could show me what she was like," she said eventually, moving so that she now faced Jake. "From a photograph, like the ones in the house. But they can't show me what I missed, for all those years. Not what she would have been. And even if they could, I don't want to know what I missed, it would break my heart. And it wouldn't be fair on Duncan, to have that image in my mind. Of an ideal mum, who wasn't there for me. Because Duncan *has* been there, always."

A single tear fell on Alva's cheek, which she wiped away. "It was different for Ruan," she said. "He and Eileen had had their whole lives together. But it's better for me if Mum stays in the photos. Does that make sense?"

It did. Not just that, it also put a different slant on Alva and Duncan's relationship. Jake had only ever seen the bickering. The eye-rolls, the exasperation. He hadn't seen the love.

Alva shifted in her seat, turning away from him. "Look," she said.

High up, to the north, the night sky was changing. Flashes of light gave way to an onslaught of colour. A luminous green streak spread steadily across the horizon, with a vivid pink and deep purple above. At the outer edges, the curtains of light twisted and soared, while in the higher planes distant stars winked in the black beyond.

"Wow," said Jake.

"You never seen the northern lights before, *sassenach*?" Alva grinned at him, indulgently.

"Is that what they are?"

Jake stood up, under a sky that pulsed with colour. Streaks and swirls reached down and obscured the tops of the distant hills on the mainland, while the water in the sound reflected back the rippling light.

He'd never seen anything like it. Another miracle that the universe had thrown at him – another phenomenon that he couldn't explain.

Ask me again, Alva. Ask me what I've got to stay for. Because the reasons seemed to be piling up.

Chapter 35

The next afternoon, Monday, Jake was at the hotel helping Alva prep for the evening dinner service.

They'd had a moment, the night before, hadn't they? He was almost certain of it, but then again, he wasn't the best at judging these situations.

It's not like he'd *never* had a girlfriend, but equally, as his cricket-mad mate, Seth, had said, reaching for an analogy, he didn't tend to bother the scorers that much either.

Look, girls were tricky. Especially fierce girls who blew cold and cold and only occasionally hot, and even then it was more like tepid. How was anyone supposed to know what to do when the girl you liked seemed to think you were an idiot, and that was on a good day?

Had there been a moment between them? To raise the subject or not, that was the question?

Alva chopped a carrot furiously, as though the whole of carrot-kind had offended her grievously.

OK, not. Not today, anyway.

They hadn't seen the General or his crew for over a week now, and that was surely behind the ongoing vegetable massacre.

"Oh, they'll be fine," she said. "Can stay down there for ever, according to them. Proper little self-sufficient aliens they are. Food labs. Water salination plant. Air filters. Don't need to come up at all, according to the General."

Now an onion was getting the carrot treatment. And Alva wasn't the one crying, put it like that.

"That's good, though, right?" ventured Jake. "No one's going to find them, if they stay put on board the ship?"

"Yes, I know. Obviously." Case in point. Her tone said – you idiot.

The chopped onion was tipped into a frying pan along with the diced carrot, with both veg looking at each other, going, what the hell just happened to us?

"It's just – "

She missed them. She didn't have to say it, Jake knew. He did, too, if he was honest, given that their presence was the reason he was still here. Hanging out on a faraway island, not being paid properly for a job that didn't really exist. Helping brutalise vegetables with someone he thought he liked – you know, like liked – but was a tiny bit frightened of.

And if he couldn't talk to Alva, and the aliens weren't going to be around much, then what was the point of staying?

Duncan wandered in, looking puzzled.

"I've had a missed call," he said. "On the old mobile." He waved his phone, as though it was a mystery to him that it rang now and again.

Alva reached for a bulb of garlic, which had no idea what was about to happen to it.

"So, I listened to the message."

Like all old people, Duncan seemed to be under the impression that his phone ringing, and someone leaving him a message, counted as a riveting anecdote.

"And it was the solicitor," he continued. If that was the punchline, Jake could tell him now, it wasn't going to cut it with Alva, the mood she was in.

"What is it, Duncan, I'm busy?"

"The solicitor, Alva darling."

"Don't darling me. What do I care about your solicitor?"

"Well, apparently he wants to talk to you. He left his number."

In went the garlic. Chopped, crushed, bewildered.

"Out of my kitchen, Duncan." She brandished the knife at him. "I know, you're going to sell, you've told me a million times. I don't need him telling me as well what a marvellous thing it is for the island. You do what you want, I'm beyond it now. Past caring."

"But Alva – "

"Out!"

Duncan made the sensible choice and retreated. And Jake, equally sensibly, did what he was told for the rest of the afternoon, as various root vegetables and cuts of meat met hideous ends.

At around five-thirty, Duncan put his head around the kitchen door again. He was holding his phone out before him.

Brave man.

"Erm, Alva darling, it's your auntie, wants a quick word."

Alva raised an eyebrow. "Morag?" She wiped her hands on her apron and looked at the clock. "All right. Give it here."

Duncan handed her the phone, turned for the door, and gave Jake the nod of a man who's just done something he thinks is very clever.

"Who is this?" Alva was peering at the number on the phone, and then put it back to her ear. She listened to the reply. "I see," she said, and fixed Fraser with a glare. In his shoes, Jake would start running now, try and get a head start.

There was another long pause as the solicitor, presumably, held forth. At one point, Alva leaned back against a wall. "I don't understand," she said, and then, finally, "Thank you, bye."

She handed the phone back to Duncan.

"Well?"

"He's Ruan's solicitor, too, it turns out."

"I know," said Duncan. "I got him from old man Strang originally, Ruan's father. Stickler for business, he was. Said this fella was good. What did he want? He wouldn't tell me."

Alva coughed, cleared her throat. "Seems like Ruan put me in his will."

"He did?" That took Duncan aback, who then rallied. "Well, of course he did. All that you did for him over the last couple of years, makes sense. Nice little keepsake, is it? Or is it a bit of money?"

Jake could see Duncan's cogs whirring at the prospect of a few hundred pounds going into the family kitty. Good luck to him if he thought Alva was going to share that.

"It's not just money," she said.

"How do you mean?"

"It's not only a bit of money."

"Not one of those god-awful paintings? Old man Strang always reckoned he had an eye for art. I think they saw him coming. Sorry, love. Still, a bit of money's nice. Help with college, you know, when you go back."

Alva shook her head. "No," she said.

"Of course," said Duncan, hurriedly. "No rush, whenever you think you're ready." He grimaced at Jake, hadn't meant to put his foot in it.

She sighed and shook her head again. "He's left me everything," she said. "He didn't have any other family. The solicitor said he changed his will six months ago. Money, shares, the house, the land, the lot. It's all mine."

____

Chapter 36

____

Jake stood in front of a swirling landscape of choppy waters, rock pools and scudding white clouds.

"This thing? Are you sure?"

"That's what the solicitor said. It's a McTaggart, apparently."

"Is that good?"

"I don't know if it's good, exactly." Alva squinted at the oil painting and then at a sheet of paper in her hand. "Not really my thing. But it's worth thirty thousand, more or less."

"What!"

"The solicitor emailed an inventory. It's all on here."

They sat back on the sofa in Ruan's lounge and contemplated Alva's inheritance. It was considerably more than a bit of money and a god-awful painting. There were four other McTaggarts on the wall in front of them, two more in a bedroom, and a Samuel Peploe in the corridor. They hadn't even looked in the other rooms yet. The art alone was worth over a quarter of a million.

In fact, the sofa and TV were the only things in the lounge that weren't worth anything, although Alva reckoned they could probably get an Edinburgh hipster to buy the video-player. The geometric rug beneath their feet – speckled with sand from the beach and spattered with Ruan's whisky – was authentic 1920s' Persian, another ten grand at auction thought the solicitor. Jake heard the figure and lifted his feet hastily.

"Like Duncan said, Ruan's dad was a bit of a collector. And a canny businessman."

"And yet Ruan lived like this?" Jake gestured around him at the piled-up newspapers, the half-completed jigsaws, the dust on the floral jugs on the sideboard – sorry, the hand-painted, ceramic Wemyss-ware, five hundred quid a pop.

"*They* lived like this, him and Eileen, like his parents before him. They were cosy here. Comfortable. It was just inherited furniture and family stuff to them. After she died, I suppose he never even thought about what it was worth. It was familiar. Reminded him of her."

The oak table, scratched by alien talons. Dining chairs, ditto. Sideboard, sticky with spilled whisky. Plus, wardrobes and dressing tables. Footstools and chests. Carved beds. Mirrors. Vases. Antique figurines. There was a figure attached to each item on Alva's list, and it added up to a lot.

"Bloody hell."

"That's only the contents. House and land – hang on, it's here at the bottom…" She scanned down and read out, "… in current market conditions, could realise two and a half million pounds."

Jake was dumbfounded.

"Not that I'm selling the house or the land."

"Well, no, obviously. Still, that's a lot of money, just from the stuff in the house."

"Oh, there's more." Alva winked at him. Actually winked. "Would you like to know about the investment bonds, sale of shares, and bank accounts?"

"Do you know, I rather think I would."

She turned the page over and brandished it at Jake, who couldn't understand what he was seeing at first, because there seemed to be a list of numbers culminating in a bold, underlined figure that said, '**£2,000,000 (two million pounds)**,' and obviously that couldn't be right.

"Oh my god. That's insane. Does Duncan know?"

"He doesn't, not yet. He thinks I've been left the house and a dodgy old painting or two. And he's no idea what the house is worth. But you know what this means?"

"That you're a millionaire? Jesus."

"A multi-millionaire, if you please." Alva was more energised and upbeat than he'd seen her in weeks. Ever, in fact – energised and upbeat not being the first adjectives he'd reach for if asked to describe Alva. "And not that, no. It means we're safe. They're safe. It's my house and land now. No one can buy it. No one can come here without permission."

She beamed at Jake. Actually beamed. First the winking, now the beaming. It was hugely disconcerting.

"Aren't you forgetting the hotel? Someone's still going to buy that." Jake didn't like to rain on her parade, but in her excitement about the money and the house, it seemed like she had taken her eye off the greatest threat to the Trogirans. The fact that the new owners of the hotel would be going all out to attract visitors to the island.

"I am not, Jakey-boy."

Jakey-boy? Who was this person, and what had they done with Alva? Was there some kind of Trogiran body-swap procedure he didn't know about?

"Someone *is* going to buy the hotel," she continued. "Me. I've got tons of money, haven't you heard?" She waved the piece of paper at him, jauntily.

"But Duncan and Jimmy have got a buyer? The hotel group?"

"I'll outbid them. Duncan won't care, as long as he gets the money. And he won't have to pay that shifty agent, Armstrong, a commission, so he'll be delighted. And I can sure as hell control what they do with the place once I own it. Keep any changes nice and small. Maybe make it a community centre instead?"

As she paced around the room, outlining possibilities, Jake wanted to believe that it was all so simple. That the heavens – luck, fate – had provided a solution.

She did have the money, that much was true.

Maybe she could damp down Duncan's flights of economic fantasy? Put some money into the village and its amenities; keep the place alive without selling out to tourism. Keep everything hidden, everyone safe.

But for how long? And at what cost? To protect the Trogirans, Alva would have to stay here for as long as they did. Never leave Elsay. Spend her fortune to try and keep them safe.

And it still might not be enough. It would only take a single wandering tourist to happen upon the beach one day, as the wee fellas were emerging, and that would be that. Game over.

In his heart of hearts, Jake had never imagined that they could keep something like this a secret forever. It wasn't Area 51, guarded by elite-force troopers, just a tiny Scottish island with a general store that sold water pistols.

"I still can't really believe it!"

Alva was clearly in full-on celebration mode, high on adrenaline. It was the only thing that could explain what happened next, namely the throwing of the arms around his shoulders, the big hug, and the squarely planted kiss on his cheek. No longer distrustful-of-strangers, *Zombieland* Emma Stone. No, this was full-on *Crazy, Stupid, Love* Emma Stone.

She withdrew as quickly as she'd dived in. "Don't mind me, bit carried away."

"Sure, no problem. Sorry."

Sorry? Why did he say *that*? He didn't mind in the slightest.

A tapping at the front door interrupted the slightly awkward silence, and they looked at each other in alarm.

No one ever came to the house, apart from them. No one *should* be coming to the house. Had they left the gate across the road open? Jake didn't think so – they were always very careful.

There was more tapping, and a harrumphing sound from outside that was vaguely familiar. Alva opened the door to find the General hovering at door-knocker height, clearly exasperated because his eyebrows were flaring.

"How the devil does this infernal door work? This lever refuses to engage the automatic slide mechanism. Ah, swings open like that, does it? Shoddy workman-ship. Sassnack tradesman, no doubt. Ah, Lady Alva, there you are! Capital."

"What are you doing out of the ship?" she said. Gimlet glare, both barrels; welcome back, classic Alva. "That's so dangerous, anyone might have seen you."

It was a good question. The Trogirans never came up to the house on their own, not without Alva or Jake checking first that it was safe and then calling them up on their video intercom.

"And how did you get out of the boatshed?" said Jake, thinking out loud. Alva had the only key to the land-side door.

"Yes, well, the chaps might have had to neutralise that, I'm afraid. Couldn't wait, very important." The General looked down at a team of half a dozen of his crew, wands drawn, standing in a defensive formation below him, scanning the nearby woods.

"Quick, get in, for god's sake. Before someone sees you."

Alva shooed them inside and closed the door. The General and his team fluttered around and came to settle on the back of the sofa, though a couple took up a flanking position on top of the dining table. Jake winced. More scratches. Another fifty quid off the sale price.

"Well, now you're here, I can tell you my news I suppose," said Alva. "It's very good news actually."

"I'm going to stop you there, Lady Alva. The news from your planet, fascinating though I'm sure it is, must wait. I have come post-haste from our surveillance unit, which has received a signal from the relay antenna that Science Officer Hvar installed in Lord Strang's vessel chamber. Never expected that to work myself, as you know, but our chaps are certain. Boffins, you know, double-checked everything, all tickety-boo as far as they're concerned. Rather an emotional time, to tell the truth." The General dabbed at an eye.

"What on earth are you talking about?"

"The fleet is here, Lady Alva. We thought it lost, and they us. Even with the new quantum scanner of Hvar's, it seemed impossible that we would ever find each other again. But against all odds, they have made contact. It seems we are saved."

"What?"

"Of course," said the General, "I'm simply the

chap in charge of the vessel. Don't profess to understand all the science, that's why we have the boffins, eh?" He snorted. "Odd chaps, don't you know – still, bless their white tunics and eyeglasses, they spotted the significance of the lights straight away, and the antenna signal confirmed it. It'll be the training, I suppose."

"I don't understand," said Alva. "What lights?"

"Well, I don't have a boffin with me to explain it, as you can see. Very difficult to persuade them to leave their station. But, in as much as I understand it…"

The lights? As the General talked on, getting closer to an explanation, for once Jake was one step ahead of Alva.

It seemed that, save for General Zadar's missing vessel, the Trogiran exodus fleet had remained intact. Crisscrossing the galaxy, seeking sanctuary, until one day receiving distant word from the Kotor System, their home, that the Niksic had been defeated. Their neighbours and allies had finally risen up, the enemy decimated and driven back to the outer rim.

"We had no idea, of course," said the General. "Not until the fleet jumped homewards, via an uncharted system, and detected an anomalous signal from a rocky planet."

Earth. Third closest planet to the system's star. The Sun. From where a hidden Trogiran vessel, under several hundred feet of water in a Scottish loch, had been broadcasting a masked emergency signal.

"… arrival of the fleet… disturbance in the electromagnetic force… some transient local interference… all now tickety-boo, as I said…"

The General was still warbling on, hopping from foot to foot as he spoke.

"That was the fleet?" said Jake, cutting in. "The colours in the sky? The fuzzy TV reception? Not the Northern Lights at all?"

"By Jove," said the General, with the tone of someone who'd just seen a budgie solve an algebraic expression. "I wasn't aware you had undergone the scientific training yourself? Remarkable. But yes, the fleet is in place and contact has been made. We will be mobilising imminently."

"Mobilising?" said Alva, shaking her head, still not getting it.

"We are returning home, Lady Alva. To Trogir. I am assuming command of our fleet once again, and we return to rebuild, with the help of our friends and neighbours."

————————————

Chapter 37

————————————

The colour drained from Alva's face, as she slowly took on board what the General was saying.

"No."

The General heard the disbelief in her voice but didn't read the reason.

"It's quite so, Lady Alva. We're shocked, too, of course. But we're ready. We've always been ready, thanks to the valiant support that you and the late Lord Strang have provided."

"But you'll be safe here now!" Alva looked almost frantic. She explained about the money, and how the threat of discovery had receded.

"And Agent Armstrong vanquished, you say? We were going to neutralise the blighter for you as a parting gift, but I suppose that won't be necessary now." He exchanged glances with his crew who looked disappointed at the news.

"You can't leave," she said, plaintively, and sat down

heavily on the sofa, the corner of one eye wet with tears. Jake sat beside her, debating for a moment or two whether to do it or not, and then threw caution to the wind and took her hand in his. She barely seemed to notice.

"They have to," he said, gently. He didn't want it to be true, either, but he had seen the excitement in the General's face.

The General fluttered forward, pirouetted in the air, and touched down softly on Alva's knees, facing her.

"We must, Lady Alva," he said. Jake had never heard him speak so tenderly. "We always hoped this day would come, and we have been away too long. Our home awaits." The General reached out and gently brushed a tear from Alva's face with the back of his taloned claw. "And you, m'lady, must assume your inheritance and keep the Strang lands safe for ever more. I have my duty, and that is yours."

He nodded at her encouragingly, and Alva looked into his eyes and gave a slight nod of her own.

"When will you go?" she said.

"As soon as the boffins have finished the pre-flight checks and coordinated jump plans with the fleet. Within the next 24 hours, I'm informed."

"So soon?" She slumped a little again.

"But not before we conclude our business here, Lady Alva. I wanted to see you in person, of course, to explain the situation. The least I could do, after all your kindness. And I brought some of the chaps along, as you see."

The other half-dozen Trogirans, who had been shuffling impatiently while the General had been talking, hopped to the ground and snapped to attention. Dressed identically, as always, with the same flyaway eyebrows and bushy facial hair as the General.

Yet now, after several weeks, Jake was beginning to identify the small differences that set them apart – a patch of grey here, an extra tuft there, some distinctive colouring on their skin. He recognised the ones he had heard addressed as the sergeant and the lieutenant, and perhaps another one or two as well. Did they have names? Families? Loved ones? He still didn't know, and never would.

"Now, our first task was to have been to deal with Agent Armstrong. Are you sure we can't give him a taste of Trogiran steel?"

The six crew members bristled, and presented arms, eager to serve. Alva smiled and shook her head.

"No, right-ho, as you wish. Disappointing. On to the second task then." The General waved a claw and one of the crew stepped forward, reaching inside their tunic and pulling out a thin tube. This rolled out into a flexible, rectangular sheet about a foot wide, which they held aloft, above their head.

The General tapped the sheet with his baton and it lit up like a screen, showing a star map – suns, planets, swirling gas spheres, spirals and flares.

"We have been pondering how to thank our gracious hosts for their kindness, and Sergeant Tivat here came to me with an excellent suggestion."

The sergeant, both arms raised, holding the thin screen, executed a bandy-legged curtsey.

"This is our arm of the galaxy, and this is the Kotor System." The General tapped again and zoomed the view. "And here" – another tap – "is Trogir."

For the first time, Jake looked upon their home planet. A pale dot, an unimaginable distance away.

The General tapped again and the view zoomed out, so that the dot disappeared amid a sea of stars.

"This is the view from Trogir as we gaze to the skies. We have many, many visible stars, as you can see, a large number of which are known only by their numerical designation. By my authority, and with the agreement of the fleet, the twin stars here shall henceforth be known as 'Strang' and 'Alva.' They shall watch over us as we rebuild. They will be our guiding lights."

The General tapped one last time, and the two stars winked in unison. Alva gulped and cleared her throat. Overwhelmed, she took a moment to reply.

"I don't know what to say. That's beautiful. Thank you, General."

Sergeant Tivat lowered his arms, rolled the screen back to a tube, and presented it to Alva.

"The thanks are all ours, Lady Alva. The screen will respond to your touch. Keep it safe, and may it always be seen as a tribute to your selfless devotion to the Trogiran cause."

The sergeant stepped back in line, to be replaced by another of the crew, who withdrew a baton from a side holster and handed it reverently to the General, who had now hopped down from Alva's knees.

He touched the catch on the side of the baton and extended it, and then held it before him, turning it slightly, this way and that. Unlike the ones Jake had seen before, this lance had a carved hilt and was marked with symbols that glowed, even in the room's morning light.

"You sir, on your knees." The General turned to Jake and intimated that he should get off the sofa. "Yes, man, there! Be quick about it, we haven't got all day."

With a couple of prods from muttering Trogirans, Jake was manoeuvred into a kneeling position before the General. The small alien looked up, holding the lance steady with two hands, somewhere around Jake's left ear.

"Lord Strang informed me on the day we met of your shortcomings. A Sassnack interloper. Missing whiskers. Impertinence. Damned lucky you weren't neutralised there and then, if you ask me. But you have proved yourself a loyal servant to Lady Alva – "

Jake started to protest, but the General silenced him with a twitch of the lance. "A loyal servant," he repeated, emphasising the final word with a hard stare, "and a true friend to the Trogiran people. Your bravery during Lord Strang's last battle should also not be over-looked. For these reasons, I take the Trogiran ceremonial wand – "

Jake tried his best not to laugh, while the General wielded the lance, tapping each shoulder.

"And dub you, Duke Jake, defender of the Strang lands of Planet Earth. You may rise."

Jake, still fighting a smile, made as if to get up, though the General stopped him briefly with a claw on his shoulder, and whispered into ear. "And grow some damned whiskers, man! Really, very poor show for a nobleman."

The General retracted the ceremonial wand and handed it back. And then he and his six companions rose in the air with a silent flutter, and hovered in formation in front of Alva and Jake.

"Is this really it?" Alva held out her hands. "You're definitely leaving?"

"It is farewell, Lady Alva. It is our destiny. But we shall never forget you."

"Then good luck," she said. "You changed our lives. You'll never know how much. I don't know what we're going to do now." She looked around the room helplessly.

"Door!" commanded the General, one final time. Jake realised that the order was for him and moved to open it. He'd give the little squirt one last ducal service.

"Oh, come here, you," said Alva, and leaned forward and grasped the General in a hug, kissing him on what was presumably a cheek, somewhere under the beard.

"Most irregular," harrumphed the General, and while Jake had never seen an alien blush, he had no doubt that was what was going on, having been on the receiving end of a cheek-kiss himself recently.

And with a final salute, they were gone – peeling out of the door, one after the other, the General bringing up the rear. They dipped and swooped for the short distance from the house to the trees at the top of the glen, and disappeared into the woods. There was a flap and a squawk as a couple of birds erupted from branches, alarmed at the passing group.

Alva stood at the door for a moment, looking into the distance, and then shook her head, as if clearing her thoughts.

"Come on," she said, and started to run.

Jake followed her down the path and into the woods. There were no sounds of flight ahead of them, and all Jake could hear was the pounding of their feet as they tore through the trees and emerged onto the sand a couple of minutes later.

The beach was clear and they crossed it quickly, jumping onto the pier and heading for the boathouse. Pieces of wood were scattered all around – the neutralised door, if the gaping hole was anything to go by.

They pulled up inside, panting, and looked around.

The Trogirans were gone. Back to their ship.

The elevator chute, complete with video link to an alien vessel, had disappeared, too. Retracted? Destroyed? It was impossible to say – it was if it had never been there.

There was only the lapping water at the foot of the pier, and the dark, impenetrable depths below.

Chapter 38

Jake walked up the harbour road and stopped at the water's edge. It was another warm day on Elsay, though for once the sun was partially obscured by a bank of high cloud.

A weather-beaten figure balancing a stack of flat plastic crates was struggling to board a moored fishing boat, and Jake stepped in to help. He slid a couple of crates off the top, unbalancing the man, who stumbled – the entire stack clattering to the deck.

"Tadger," said Dougie Crowther, straightening up, seeing who it was.

"Sorry, Dougie, just trying to help." Jake might have known. The painter and decorator also owned a fishing boat, of course he did. "Want me to pick them up for you?"

"Walloper," said Dougie, waving him away, which Jake took to mean – no, you're all right, but thanks.

Something like that, anyway. You couldn't always be sure with Dougie.

Outside the general store, Mrs Dunmore was arranging a display of apples, pears and grapes on a sloping shelf. She'd already wheeled out a rack of post-cards and a rather more hopeful carousel of death-metal CDs. The Saturday ferry would be in shortly, so she was getting ready for the few day-trippers who might make their way up the few miles to the village.

"Tally ho! dearie," she said, as Jake passed by. "How's it going with Alva?" Mrs Dunmore had taken a highly personal interest in the pair of them, which Jake found endearing if a little unnerving, but on this occasion she didn't wait for an answer. Not that there was an answer that would satisfy her, short of Jake announcing that the wedding was next Tuesday. "Looks like rain, of all things," she said.

Jake looked out over the harbour, into the sound beyond, where the sky had darkened further.

"I might even sell one of these, what do you think?" Mrs Dunmore twinkled at him, twirling a pink unicorn umbrella emblazoned with Japanese characters. Jake had wondered where those had gone. Duncan had obviously been unloading unsold stock; he hoped Mrs D had driven a hard bargain.

Outside the hotel, Jake spotted Bangkok Ewan up a ladder and gave it a friendly shake, copping an earful of abuse in return. Thank god it wasn't him having to clean the gutters. Instead, Duncan had made an irresistible offer to Bangkok, who was grumbling, even so, as he scraped a trowel along the half-pipe and emptied debris into a dangling bucket.

Jimmy was standing in the doorway of the public bar, directing operations. Jake gave him a careful nod. He still didn't think he was entirely in the clear about the damaged Land Rover – that perhaps Jimmy was biding his time to exact his full revenge, though to be honest, being made to drink the Little Widdle was punishment enough.

"Duncan inside?"

"Up at the house," said Jimmy. "He said to send you up there, he's got a job for you."

Jake knew what the job was. It was almost certainly to do with Alva. Duncan deciding that she needed cheering up again. Or maybe taking over from her at the souvenir shop, if she didn't feel like working there today. Jake guessed that's the last thing she felt like doing.

The previous day, he had driven her back from Ruan's house – her house now – in silence after the Trogirans had said their goodbyes.

The two of them had stood in the boathouse for a while, gazing out of the open end into the loch, as if they might see a ripple, a bubble, anything that signified the General and his crew disappearing for one last time down into the ship.

There had been nothing. And Alva had wept quietly as he led her back up the beach, through the glen and into the house. They'd got into Duncan's van and Jake had driven her home, dropping her off at the house on the hill under the castle.

"I'll be fine," she had said. "It's a lot to take in – that they're not going to be here anymore. I'm going to miss them. Miss – everything, you know?"

Jake understood. He'd only known about the Trogirans for two months. She'd had two years with them. It was hard to see how you could go back to normal life, when you knew what was out there in the universe – and when you knew that you couldn't tell anyone, or that even if you did, no one would believe you. That was a different kind of burden to bear, and one he'd have to get used to now as well.

Better go and see what Duncan wanted.

Jake left Bangkok and Jimmy to it on the quayside, Bangkok now fretting that it looked like as if it was going to pour with rain. Jake could hear Jimmy encouraging him to work faster if he didn't want to get soaked. Which, apparently, wasn't the sort of assistance Bangkok was looking for, and why didn't Jimmy bugger off inside and fetch him a pint, if he wasn't actually going to help clean his own hotel.

Jake walked back past the village shop and waved at Mrs Dunmore, now settled into a camping chair outside her shop, brolly at the ready. And he set off on the winding road up the hill towards the Fraser house.

On the last bend, Jake turned to look down at the harbour. Dougie still stacking crates on his boat, a couple of gulls circling overhead. The woods away to the right, cliffs to the left. The open water beyond, with the distant hills of the mainland just about visible on the horizon.

A couple of cyclists freewheeled along the harbour-side and paused by a bench. The ferry must be in. Early customers – Fraser would be gutted if the shop stayed closed.

More high cloud had rolled in and while it had stayed warm, the skies had darkened even further. There was a distant rumble, too. Mrs D might clean up today if she was lucky. That would really piss Duncan off, because Jake knew he hadn't sold a single one of those pink umbrellas.

He'd miss this, if he left – the village, the view, the hotel bar, even some of the people. Especially some of the people. One person, anyway.

Was that what he was thinking of doing? Leaving? He didn't know for certain. But it was as Alva had said to him, not so long ago. He couldn't stay forever. He'd go back sometime, to home, to college. Maybe it was time, now the Trogirans had gone?

Duncan opened the door the second he rapped on it, like he'd been waiting for him.

"Good man, come in. I've got a bit of a situation, but she's outside on the terrace. Have a word with her, will you? See if she's going down to the shop today? Otherwise, you'll have to do it, all right?"

Duncan darted back to the lounge, where he had the TV pulled away from the wall, cables everywhere.

"Bloody thing," he said. "Still can't get a picture out

of it, and now the electricity's gone off. Bloody weather."

He disappeared into the kitchen, and Jake could hear the up-down click of fuses being switched on and off, accompanied by exasperated swearing.

Jake slid open the French doors. The sky had changed again during his short walk up the house. Almost bruised now, with flashes in the distance and then more rumbling. No rain yet, but it was surely coming.

Alva stood by the bench, a little way down in the garden. She had her back to the house, looking out over the water and didn't hear him approach.

"All right?" said Jake, touching her arm.

She turned towards him, with a look he hadn't seen before. Wide eyes, open expression. "You're here," she said – and for once it didn't sound accusatory.

"Your dad says – "

"Listen."

Alva tapped the side of her face, near her ear.

"And look." She pointed up at the sky.

The clouds were now deep blue and a vivid purple, while green and red streaks pulsed downwards and the rumbling turned into a muffled roar.

"What?" said Jake, though he knew.

"It's them. Can't you hear it?"

And now he did – a low crackle that he'd thought was something in the air, something to do with the approaching storm.

Only it wasn't a storm, and the crackle was in his

head, between his ears. Where there was a communication device and transmitter, placed there by small aliens so that he could hear and understand them.

"What's happening?" he said.

"The fleet. They're coming for them," said Alva, her eyes shining.

Chapter 39

There was no blue sky or natural daylight left on this summer's day in late July. A flashing, rolling, dancing, multicoloured shroud stretched above them as far as the eye could see, like they were under a vast tent festooned with winking fairy lights.

The crackling sound in Jake's ear resolved itself into a background fuzz of white noise, like a long, whispered shush. Then it stopped and, clear as a bell, Jake heard the General's voice.

"Fleet, assemble!"

Alva clapped her hands in joy – she'd heard it too – and they both stared into the sky. Out of the corner of his eye, Jake saw that Duncan had come out into the garden. Standing there, gawping, mystified. Welcome to our world, pal.

There was a loud whump – not in his ears, from up in the sky – and all the air seemed to be sucked out of the atmosphere. Jake felt the hairs prickle on his arms and neck. A deep silence fell over the village, the harbour and the open water beyond.

And the boiling, flashing clouds simply vanished.

High above, in the blue skies of a summer's day, under a beating sun, stretched a stationary fleet of alien spaceships. Classic saucer shape, with a lower bulge and a sprinkling of upper towers. Some larger, almost like floating tankers. Others smaller and more streamlined.

Too high to gauge size, too many to count, they stretched on and on in a loose formation that disappeared into distant clouds. Hundreds of them, holding the returning population of an entire planet in the Kotor System, billions of miles away across the universe.

Alva pointed again. Out on the water, well beyond the harbour and past the entrance to the loch, perhaps a mile up the coast, spouts were shooting from the sea. The water frothed and churned, and a vast, dark, swirling patch appeared, drawing the water down in a sort of whirlpool effect.

The clicking noise returned in Jake's ear for a few seconds before cutting out completely – and a circular ship rose slowly from the sound, water draining off the sides as it climbed higher. Coloured lights showed on its lower part, flashing a repeating pattern.

Alva hugged him in glee and then turned back, not wanting to miss a second of it.

Jake just stared, not even feeling the hug.

The ship. The General's vessel. Exactly where Alva and Ruan had said it was, not to mention the Trogirans themselves. He'd doubted it for so long, and yet there it was.

Duncan had walked down to stand beside them. Staggered was probably the better word – he stood there, gripping the back of the bench for balance, shaking his head in disbelief. Jake could hardly blame him.

It wouldn't just be Duncan though, would it? Half the village had been out this morning, and the rest had surely emerged from their houses by now. Not to mention the visitors off the ferry. And probably half of Scotland as well. That light-show must have been visible for miles, and now there was a fleet of alien ships crowding the sky above Elsay. If Bangkok hadn't fallen off his ladder, it would be a miracle.

"That's torn it," he said to Alva. "So much for keeping it a – "

"Ssh," she said, gesturing at Duncan, who was lost in open-mouthed amazement. Jake reckoned he could show a PowerPoint presentation about the alien visitation on Elsay to Duncan right now, and he wouldn't notice, but he took her point.

"Let's watch," she whispered.

The General's ship had risen a couple of hundred feet above the water and come to a halt. It was bigger than Jake had expected, though that could be the relative scale, because it hovered far below the fleet which had come for it. Those ships sat there still, high in the sky, waiting in their ranks.

The lights on the General's ship continued to pulse

in different colours, in a sequence of five. There was a loud blast of sound, followed by a ripple of musical notes which echoed across the island as the ship started to spin slowly, like an untethered revolving restaurant.

Five notes, different tones but repeated in the same pattern – sometimes faster, sometimes slower – booming from the ship, rising in volume, ricocheting off the nearby hills. The rising, tumbling jumble of tones and half-tones of a runaway church organ. Jake could hear the simple melody within, and could hear gulls squawking in alarm, but he just laughed. He knew those notes, that simple tune. Everyone did.

"What's so funny?" said Alva, smiling. Laughing with him at the absurdity of it – the sound, the spectacle.

"*Close Encounters*," he said.

She looked blank.

"The film, *Close Encounters of the Third Kind?*"

She shrugged.

How could you be with someone who didn't know *Close Encounters?* He'd have to worry about that later.

Be with someone? He'd worry about that, too.

"It's a message," he whispered. "They're saying goodbye."

The bloody General. He'd probably found the video in Strang's house. Had a sense of humour after all.

The notes died away. Silence enveloped the island once again, save for some distant car alarms that must have been set off by the electromagnetic charge in the air. A dog was going crazy somewhere, too. He could hear Duncan beside him, almost gasping for air.

Alva found Jake's hand and they stood there, gazing into the sky at the secret they had tried so hard to keep. Now the biggest open secret in the world – but not caring about that in the most remarkable of shared moments.

And then the fleet disappeared. Winked out, as one, jumping for home, leaving only the blue sky and wispy, white clouds of a normal summer's day.

The General's ship lingered a moment more, but was then on the move, rising higher before soaring in an ascending circle. It got smaller and smaller as it climbed and then it too vanished – although for a long minute afterwards, Jake strained his eyes, looking for even a speck in the sky.

There was nothing.

Nothing to say they'd ever been here.

They were gone.

Alva had dropped her gaze before Jake and leaned into him, putting an arm around his waist. She was still smiling, he could see. More than smiling. Beaming.

Relief? Vindication? Either way, he had a feeling she would be all right.

And he had a decision to make.

Alva stepped away and looked at him.

"Now what?" she said.

Chapter 40

'Hundreds of visitors are expected to descend this week on the Scottish island of Elsay to celebrate the one-year anniversary of the extraordinary sightings above this small settlement. Scientists are still divided about what happened that day – alien visitation, atmospheric mirage or mass hysteria? – but the people flocking to Elsay are in no doubt, and are hoping for a sign from the skies.'

Jake was at the Elsay ferry landing, waiting with the bus driver as the passengers streamed off. The daily ferry service had been restored a few months ago; the bus was Duncan's idea. Starting as he meant to go on, by dropping them right outside the gift shop – the 'going on' being to make as much money as possible before the bubble burst.

Not that the bubble showed any sign of bursting.

Jake held up his sign and directed the visitors on board. The usual full bingo card —homemade 'Welcome' signs, saucer-eyed alien masks, antenna headbands, painted faces, green onesies, black robes and silver arm-gloves.

Not a bearded, bushy-faced, wing-tipped gremlin-fairy among them, which was always a relief to Jake. It meant their secret was still safe.

He'd grown a beard himself, shortly after the Trogirans had left, remembering what General Zadar had told him – and also thinking it would be a laugh.

Alva had just said, "What are you doing, that's awful?" for the first few days. And when, after a couple of weeks, he had announced that this was his beard, and this is how it looked, she had simply said, "No," and that was that. Off it came again.

The people on the bus were staying at the Castle View, in freshly painted rooms and dorms both in the main house and staff quarters. Jake, Bangkok and others had been busy over the previous winter and spring as interest had slowly picked up and then exploded as the anniversary neared. The few rooms at the Port Hotel – also given a makeover – had been full for days.

Duncan even had people crammed into his own house, on the hill under the castle. He had sold it as a 'Premium Event Package' – a viewpoint from the terrace garden where he had witnessed the phenomenon with his own eyes. Two nights, inclusive of meals at the hotel, a thousand quid a head – no refunds in the event of an alien no-show.

Jake and Alva were confident about that, if nothing else. The Trogirans were long gone, and no one on Earth – barring them – even knew that they had been in the first place.

Of course, there had been attempts to find out.

Once the first photographs and videos emerged of the spectacle, the police had travelled over from the mainland and sealed off the quayside, only to discover that there wasn't anything to see. And not much to be gleaned from the likes of Dougie, Mrs Dunmore, Bangkok, Jimmy and the rest of the hotel regulars, who were as nonplussed as anyone else. Although, even if Dougie had shaken hands with an alien and had the secrets of the universe revealed to him, no one was ever going to be able to decipher them.

A couple of days later an unmarked black car had rolled off the ferry and driven slowly up to the village, where two men and two women in dark shirts, combats and trainers proceeded to take a closer interest in the surroundings.

Jake had heard the crackle of a shoulder-mic from one of them – "X-Team, report status" – and had subsequently done his best to avoid them. He didn't know what the X-Team was, but suspected it might be very interested to know that there were two people on Elsay who could definitely help with their enquiries.

He and Alva had got used to keeping a straight face whenever the 'visitors' were discussed. As far as everyone on the island was concerned, they'd all seen the phenomenon at the same time, for the first time. But Jake wasn't sure how he'd hold up to more rigorous questioning by people who looked like they believed the truth was out there.

And if they suspected he'd had first contact with an alien race, and scanned him for evidence – x-rayed him, whatever – would they be likely to find a tiny, pill-shaped, alien comms device somewhere between his ears? In which case, the scanning might well turn into probing, and Jake could live without that, so he had made himself scarce until the unmarked car and its blank-faced occupants left a few hours later.

———

The bus unloaded on the quayside, where Duncan was already in place, standing outside the gift shop.

"Here we go, Mads," he said, as the first tourists streamed through the door "Fire up the till, and don't forget to snap some photographs."

Mads. Madison. Duncan's new employee. A twenty-five-year-old stick-insect who'd turned up on the doorstep one day promising that she could increase his brand awareness in the micro-influencer souvenir scene. Duncan had lapped it all up and put her on the payroll. Jake hadn't even wanted to ask what he was paying her, given all the work he'd done virtually for free.

Mads talked in vague, vacuous riddles about the

workings of social media but was harmless enough. Remarkably, she seemed to know what she was doing, as business had never been so good. Even Alva tolerated her, on the basis that it meant she no longer had to work in the shop, while Mads herself seemed genuinely to like and get on with Duncan, which was a mystery to them all.

"Photographs, bless," said Mads. "We call it content, I've told you, Big D. Send me the maddest-looking ones and I'll get them on a live stream. We're trending in Japan right now."

Big D was new. He'd have to tell Alva, she'd love that.

"Coming tonight, Jakey boy?"

"Wouldn't miss it, Duncan." Jake raised a hand in acknowledgement, as visitors pushed past him.

Calling him Duncan was new, too, at least to his face. Jake was still getting used to saying it.

"You can't call me Mr Fraser," Duncan had said. "Not if, you know – " and he'd made some terrible, finger-linking, heart-shaped hand gesture that was supposed to represent the entirety of the decision Jake had made a year ago.

Technically, that Alva had made for him. You didn't really say no to Alva – nor, it turned out, did you want to. Not if you wanted a girlfriend, anyway. Which, much to his general amazement, is what he now had. Mrs Dunmore had been right all along.

Jake walked up to the Port Hotel and got in the Land Rover. Not Jimmy's multi-pranged Landy, but a classic Series 3 soft-top that Alva had bought for them. She didn't even mind the inevitable scratches that it had acquired over the last few months, as it had been driven up and down the track to Ruan's old house – now her house.

In fact, their house.

Although she teased him about it, it had at first been a fair question – what originally attracted you to the windfall-beneficiary, multi-millionairess, Alva Fraser?

Luckily, he had had plenty of other answers, centring on her attractiveness, intelligence, surprising kindness, and slowly emerging sense of humour. "Go on," she'd said, as he tried nervously to enumerate them, "can't you think of any more?" When he'd finally ground to a halt, she'd said, "I think you should stay, don't you? With me?" and he hadn't been able to think of a reason why not.

College would still be there – for both of them – if they ever decided they wanted to go back.

Jake's parents had been understandably concerned when he announced that he was taking a year out from his studies, but he'd badged it as a chance to take stock, to decide what he wanted to do with his life. Because it turned out that that definitely wasn't investigating representations of revolution and migration in Latin American cinema. And when that hadn't worked, he'd muttered something about needing time off for his mental health and that had shut them up.

His mates – back from America, now in their third

year at university – were desperate to come up and visit, see the famous Scottish island where aliens had appeared. They said it in a sort of woo-woo voice that suggested they didn't believe in any of it, which was fine by Jake. He'd put them off coming for now, and hadn't even told them about his relationship with Alva.

He didn't know why he'd done either of those things, but supposed he was still at the stage of working out what he thought about everything.

Ironically, the Trogirans leaving had given him even more of a reason to stay on Elsay. There was Alva, of course, that was the number-one reason – and the associated fact that she was now rich, and consequently he didn't need a paying job to keep him here.

But when it came down to it, Jake had wanted to see what happened next. The aliens might have returned to their home planet, but the island itself had undoubtedly got more interesting. Remote it might be – the last place he ever thought he'd end up living – but it was being regarded as the UK's own Roswell, and who wouldn't want to be a part of that?

Alva, meanwhile, was making good on her idea to invest in the community.

She'd bought the hotel and funded its renovation, and tried to keep a lid on Duncan's more outlandish money-making schemes. She saw an opportunity to ride the alien wave while it lasted, but was putting in place plans and investments that would benefit all the islanders, if and when the interest waned.

Although it didn't look like doing that any time soon, especially with the anniversary due.

Jake parked the Land Rover outside the house and called for Alva. The decorating was mostly finished, at least in the few rooms they were living in for now. There was another whole wing still to be renovated; outbuildings, too, if they could think of a use for them.

When she didn't answer, and he couldn't find her, Jake set off down through the glen to the beach. He knew where she'd be.

He walked softly across the sand towards the pier and boathouse, where she was sitting with her feet dangling in the water, looking out into the loch.

Where the ship had been. Where their secret had been hidden, until – 364 days ago – the General raised his vessel and set a course for Trogir and home. She still missed them. Found it hard to believe that she'd never hear from them again, but coming down here seemed to help her.

Jake sometimes found her at the house, too, with the alien map unfurled, looking at the winking star that was named after her, and the adjacent one for Strang. He loved looking at it as well, though was conscious of the fact that they wouldn't be able to explain *that* away if anyone else saw it. It was usually locked in a safe placed under their bed. A hidden secret about a hidden secret.

She was half turned away from the beach and hadn't seen him, so Jake pitched his voice slightly lower, reached for his best Duncan Fraser accent and hailed her. "Now then, darling."

"Don't you darling me," she said automatically, spinning round to see it was Jake. "Oh, it's you. Very funny."

Jake remembered all the earlier times she had said, "Oh, it's you" to him. They had never been accompanied by that smile. He'd never get tired of that smile. Like she was almost pleased to see him, he sometimes joked.

"It's me," he said. "Duncan wants to know if we're coming tonight?"

"Do we have to?"

"I think so. Anyway, you'll like it."

"It's a science-fiction film. Of course I won't like it. The tourists are bad enough, and now I have to watch a movie with them?"

"Trust me. Anyway, Duncan's already got you a costume, you can't back out now."

———

When Duncan Fraser wanted to make a buck, he certainly went all out.

"Open-air cinema," he'd said. "Gala night, you'll see."

He knew a bloke who knew a bloke, and a giant outdoor screen had turned up one day, to be erected on the quayside, with the harbour as a backdrop. It was impressive, Jake had to admit.

Mads had done whatever Mads did and a ferry-load of influencers had turned up, too. They had been skipping around the island all day looking for Insta vantage points and conducting interviews with each other. In between times, they popped into the hotel bar for highly alcoholic, dark-brown shots of something that Jimmy was calling 'Star Juice' and which Jake knew was a Beserker-and-Lidl-brandy mix.

There were seats and cushions arranged across the harbour front, and the place was packed. Had been since seven that evening; the film had started at nine, and it was now closing in on eleven. The sound echoed around the harbour, and the light from the screen lit up the cottages and hotel behind.

Alva and Jake had taken a place at the back, to one side – "Just in case," said Alva, meaning just in case she didn't want to stay for the whole thing. She'd declined Duncan's offer of a silver jumpsuit with the sort of glance that would down an alien fleet and had settled into Jake's shoulder – more resigned than interested, he'd have said.

Now, though, with maybe twenty minutes to go, she was rapt.

"See," whispered Jake, nudging her.

"Why didn't you tell me?"

"I did tell you."

"You bored me about it, film boy. That's not the same as telling."

"Wait for it," said Jake. "It gets better."

There was the low, good-natured murmur of a

couple of hundred people on the quayside watching the film, but the huge screen and projected sound was enough to draw in anyone who wanted to immerse themselves in the climax of the story.

As the five-note tonal phrase played, tentatively at first and then riotously, as human and alien conversed in the film, Alva gasped in recognition. Looked at Jake with pure joy in her face.

"Told you," he said. "General Zadar knows his classic movies. He watched enough of them."

Her face fell slightly at the mention of his name. "They're never going to come back, are they? I mean, they shouldn't. It's safer that way. But we're never going to see them again, are we?"

"No," said Jake. "I wouldn't think so. They're definitely not coming back tomorrow, whatever Duncan has promised people. We'd have heard, wouldn't we?" and he tapped his ear and smiled.

"I'm not sure he's promised anybody anything. There are asterisks and small print on anything he sends out. Say what you like about Duncan, but he's not daft."

She turned back to the screen and continued watching as the grey, human-like extra-terrestrials emerged from the mothership.

"Yeah, right," she said, perhaps more forcefully than she'd intended, "that's what aliens look like," and then she grinned at him – an 'oops' grin.

He grinned back. This was cool. Watching an outdoor movie on a Scottish island was cool. Having a girlfriend was cool. It was even cooler when you could talk in code about the biggest secret in the universe.

"It's OK, though," said Alva, leaning in close. She gestured at the crowd. "It's for the best. Can you imagine what it would be like if everyone knew the real truth? At least this way the island makes a living and no one gets hurt. And it'll all tail off eventually, and we can get back to normal."

Jake wasn't so sure, but now wasn't the time to talk about that.

Now was the time to sit back and think of absent friends with wings and wands.

To remember Ruan Strang, whose death had made Jake's new life possible.

And to watch the end of *Close Encounters of the Third Kind* with the only other person on Earth who mattered.

THE END

———

Want another Sci-Fi read? Why not grab a **free short story** introducing you to the 'Odyssey Earth' trilogy – a feelgood, character-led space opera with heart and humour.

Just scan the QR code over the page to download the free short story.

If you've just read and (I hope!) enjoyed *Third Loch From the Sun*, I have a terrible confession to make: I am sorry to say that I am undeniably English. In fact, I was born in West Africa, but I'm not sure that makes things any better, as far as writing a book set in Scotland is concerned.

But I have been to Scotland, many times, and even to some places that are a bit like my fictional island of Elsay – which, if you were looking to place it on a map, you might find somewhere west of Jura and Colonsay in the Inner Hebrides.

Everything else, I've made up too, so there's no point looking for specific locations or scenic inspirations.

However, I did once spend a week on the Isle of Mull as a student, where the folk band in the nearest pub played songs about 'murdering the English' every time we stepped through the door. And where the landlord offered to lend us his MGBGT V8 any time we wanted it. "But if you prang it," he'd say, with wild eyes – though we never found out what would happen in such an event, because we were far too scared to accept his offer.

You'll also have noticed that all the fine Scottish people portrayed in the book basically talk like English people, because there was no way I was going down the route of dialect spellings and faux Scotticisms. As Jake might say – are you mad? As an English writer, that would just be asking for trouble.

But I hope you can hear the accents, tones and intonations in all the dialogue. And I want you to rest assured that all the specifically Glaswegian comments and insults uttered by Dougie have been vetted and approved by native speakers. 'Walloper' and 'Rip ma knittin' are my absolute favourites. Obviously, though, Sassnack bampot that I am, any remaining errors are mine and mine alone.

Finally, the title. It is, of course, a riff on that great, underrated TV sitcom, *Third Rock From the Sun*, about an alien family living a regular life on Earth. I'd love to say it came to me in a flash of inspiration, because I think it's just great, but the truth is my oldest friend, John, coined it, off the top of his head and with no notice, and he obviously should be writing these books, not me. So get on to him if you're wondering when the next Sci-Fi book is due.

Like This Book?

If you enjoyed the book, please take a moment to leave me a review on Amazon, Goodreads, BookBub, or anywhere else you like.

A word or two is absolutely fine (though please, go to town if you like!), and even just a rating makes the book that much more visible to other readers.

Thanks a million – you're all stars.

About the Author

Rex Burke is a SciFi writer based in North Yorkshire, UK.

When he was young, he read every one of those yellow-jacketed Victor Gollancz hardbacks in his local library. That feeling of out-of-this-world amazement has never left him – and keeps him company as he writes his own SciFi adventures.

When Rex is not writing, he travels – one way or another, he'll get to the stars, even if it's just as stardust when his own story is done.

Find Out More

To find out more, and grab a free short story, visit Rex's website – rexburke.com